BRILLIANT

SILENCE

BRILLIANT

A book of Paragraphs
& Sentences
and 13 very, very short Stories

SILENCE

Spencer Holst

WITH "AXIAL STONES" BY GEORGE QUASHA

STATION HILL/BARRYTOWN, LTD.

Published by Station Hill / Barrytown, Ltd. in Barrytown, New York 12507.

Online catalogue and purchasing: http://www.stationhill.org

E-mail: Publishers@stationhill.org

Station Hill Arts is a project of The Institute for Publishing Arts, Inc., a not-for-profit, federally tax exempt organization in Barrytown, New York, which gratefully acknowledges ongoing support for its publishing program from the New York State Council on the Arts.

"Pleasures of the Imagination," "Text," "The Getaway Car," "Mona Lisa Meets Buddha," "The Hidden Ballroom at Versailles," "Prose for Dancing," "Brilliant Silence," "The Largest Wave in the World," "Orange," "Another Imposter," "The Cat Who Owned an Apartment," "10,000 Reflections," "The Prime Minister's Grandfather," "Miss Lady," "Chess," "The Blazing Blue Footprint," "The Purple Bird," "Real Magic," and "The Hunger of the Magicians" are reprinted from *The Zebra Storyteller*, "Miss Lady" also appeared in *Viva*. Other pieces have appeared in various periodicals including: *Scholastic Voice, Ear, East Side Review, Chelsea, Equal Time, Some/Thing, Sumac, Transition, Magazine, For Now, Prospect, Rallying Point, Green Mountain Post, Friends Seminary Review.* Stories have also appeared in numerous textbooks and anthologies including: the *Norton Introduction to Literature; Norton Introduction to Fiction; Pegasen från Prärien* (in Swedish)*; Fantastic Worlds: Myths, Tales and Stories; Self-Portrait: Book People Picture Themselves; Sudden Fiction International; Flash Fiction;* and *America a Prophecy.*

Photograph of Axial Stones on page 1 by Richard Gummere
Photographs of Axial Stones on pages 10, 14, 29-30, 44, 58, 68 by Michael Nelson
Photographs of Axial Stones on pages 73-74, 84 by George Quasha
Photographs of Spencer Holst on pages 2, 176 by Norman Saito
Cover painting by Spencer Holst
Cover design by Susan Quasha
Typesetting and Design by Susan Quasha   **3 1969 01122 9456**

Library of Congress Cataloging-in-Publication Data

Holst, Spencer.
Brilliant Silence: a book of paragraphs & sentences and 13 very, very short stories / Spencer / Holst.
p.cm.
ISBN 1-58177-055-3 (alk. paper)
I. Title
PS3558.039 B75 2000
813'.54–dc21   99-055071

Manufactured in The United States of America

Contents

The Photographs

The photographs of "Axial Stones"—that is, precariously and naturally balanced, unworked stones, using no adhesive in maintaining position—represent a series of art works by George Quasha, about which Spencer Holst writes:

"Photography can rarely do justice to works such as these by George Quasha. The Axial Stones have a reality that is far beyond what can be conveyed by pictures. Their presence here is perhaps merely evidence of the author's eloquence in pleading with the publisher for their inclusion. Seeing the stones themselves during my visit to George Quasha's house in Barrytown, New York, inspired my major new prose work published here as *Balanced Boulders*. While I have my reservations—already the stones are like old friends—I am glad to see their pictures."

Acknowledgements

The author would like to thank the people who helped with the preparation and publication of this book: Jennifer Farbar, Garry Goodrow, Margradel Hicks, Rory Baratta, Martin Mitchell, Susan Quasha and Charles Stein.

For Beate;
and
for a stranger who will read aloud, and to one
who listens—this book is dedicated; but then...
to such a pair all of literature is dedicated.

Overture for "Balanced Boulders"

TEXT BY SPENCER HOLST

FOR A MUSICAL COMPOSITION

FOR FLUTE, TUBA AND PERCUSSION

BY ROGER TRÉFOUSSE

With an easy and confident movement he lifts an elongated boulder and sets it standing upright on a large round rock, and immediately moves his hands away, and when he releases it, instead of toppling over, the upright rock remains erect with the uncanny stance that a standing stone assumes, as if its point-of-contact were engulfed by a glob of glue, frozen hard—and yet the truth is that the only glue is gravity, the gravity the truth.

An unexpected avalanche, a rockslide on Mount Fuji, leaves many boulders balanced one atop another at its base, the balanced stones in a line like an art exhibit by the god of sculpture.

On the last day of summer camp downstream from their campsite in a riverbed of boulders a hundred Boy Scouts become possessed by an idea for that final afternoon and with unbounded energy they begin to balance pairs of boulders one atop the other until they have a Boulder Show that they will never forget, a vivid vista of hundreds of pairs of balanced boulders bathed in evening sunlight—casting long shadows—a bright yellow vision to be invoked in their old age in a golden blink of total recall.

The turtle paddles upon a pond staring up at a crisp crescent moon in the deep blue sky, its neck stretched out into the air, and then it dives down and swims along the gravel bottom among the fixtures of the fish, among those uncanny pairs of stones, one balanced on the other, that sit in the sand like underwater furniture—the whole scene being the set for a Lincoln Center dance concert in which my reader takes the lead and dances the part of the turtle, the author being your audience.

A fossil of a late Cretaceous dinosaur's big toe stands out at the top of an orange rock, and astonishingly balanced on the perfectly formed toenail of the monster is another boulder of a somewhat later time, from the Tertiary Period. At the lower extremity of the second rock is a fossil of a small mammal, which stands on one foot balanced like a ballet dancer on the tip of the giant toenail. The two rocks rest in a cave protected from the changing winds of the Gobi Desert, and are discovered at the same moment and examined closely by two colleagues, archeologists, one of Beijing University, one from Harvard. The two rocks are carefully removed and they are brought back by the scientists to the Chinese university, where they now can be seen balanced at the entrance to the walled garden of the Archeology Department, under an Oriental arch, protected from the changing winds and the rain of Beijing.

Two giant gems weigh a quarter of a ton each: Three green sides meet to make three edges that themselves converge where a giant cube of jade balances on its corner in a shallow hollow of a pure ruby boulder—polished to translucent perfection—which in sunlight can cast a scarlet-tinted shadow on the floor of white Italian marble at the feet of a small dark monarch, at the foot of his gold throne in the throne room of his palace, his hereditary home, a small island on a little lake of a tiny Far Eastern kingdom, a pretty pebble plunked down in a crystal puddle among stupendous mountains of prodigious Himalayan enormity.

The Tokyo seismographs jam...but in a small and lovely public garden several pairs of balanced boulders topple, and an immediate call reporting it to a radio station—which interrupts a program to report the minor event—gives people in the great city time to remove themselves from danger of collapsing structures from seven earthquakes rated seven which follow within the hour.

Two gigantic jewels: An uncut pyramidal emerald, unclouded and the size of a small green parrot, is perched and perfectly balanced atop a perfect pearl the size of an ostrich egg, set on the surface of a large bowl of sand. Perhaps because the final bid sets a record at that London auction house—when the auctioneer cries "Sold!"—his gavel is brought down with unpremeditated violence and the emerald falls off the pearl, falls harmlessly into the sand, while onlookers gasp and the audience en masse falls into fits of infectious giggling.

After her awful operation, she balances her gallstone on her birthstone and keeps them under a bell jar on her desk at work.

A boulder is transported a great distance on an Ice Age glacier which on melting drops the erratic traveler in what is to become a Massachusetts meadow, places it precisely atop a smaller taller rock, where it remains balanced for ten thousand years. During that time the surface of the bottom rock becomes completely covered with a thick mat of dark green moss, while brilliantly colored yellow, orange, purple and red lichen grow all over the larger stone.

There is a syncopation of frogs and a noisiness of crickets in the Garden of the Goldfish Pond where pairs of balanced boulders, partially submerged, put their heads above water as if in calm appreciation of the flutey floating notes from the throats of Sooty Wastrels, which nest among the thistles in the thicket of thorns.

The cemetery for lifelong couples is a grove of balanced boulders, each double grave adorned by a pair of tombstones—of large inscribed boulders, one balanced on the other.

Balanced Boulders
384 Unconnected Paragraphs
In Six Parts

For Parker Baratta

PART ONE: 64 PARAGRAPHS

A Balanced Boulder
& 17 untitled paragraphs

With an easy and confident movement he lifts an elongated boulder and sets it standing upright on a large round rock, and immediately moves his hands away, and when he releases it, instead of toppling over, the upright rock remains erect with the uncanny stance that a standing stone assumes, as if its point-of-contact were engulfed by a glob of glue, frozen hard—and yet the truth is that the only glue is gravity, the gravity the truth.

With a perfect *snap!* he throws his fingerprints off his fingertips.

I have designed a chessboard on which squares are alternately gold and silver leaf, 16 chessmen being covered with gold and the opposing 16 men covered with silver, and it has become our best-selling and most expensive toy. We manufacture games, fancy dominoes and Chinese checkers, in a factory just outside Buffalo in a tiny town on the Canadian border, where in the distance, especially at night, the roar of Niagara Falls can be heard. A temporary worker uses this typewriter in the afternoon to knock out bills and various form letters to my customers, while in the evening after hours the Polish girl who comes in to clean uses the machine to type heavenly poems in Polish at the conclusion of her more mundane chores, and lastly, late at night, the watchman sits here working on a book about the history of the area around the Falls. This is everybody's favorite typewriter, and so it's really no surprise to discover this morning that it has been covered with gold leaf.

"Do you have a one-act play about the ghost of a dog that haunts a frail albino and his cat in a secondhand bookstore?"

He purchases a large house in Virginia which had been built before the American Revolution, and he lives in it for ten years, slowly and carefully making renovations, giving much pleasurable thought to each change he makes in the structure. He has a young architect construct an accurate floorplan of the place, and late one evening, studying it fondly before the fireplace, he realizes that there must be a secret room adjacent to the room in which he sits. On having the wall opened up, a giant clothes closet is revealed loaded with luxurious vestments, robes and clothing suitable for royalty—for, in fact, the King and Queen of America—and set securely in a double wooden hatbox are two bejeweled crowns, all in readiness should history have taken a different course.

Monet in New York is the title of the book. He painted from a New York City rooftop for three months on a clandestine visit to the city accompanied by his pretty secretary, which was a scandal. She is the author of the book. In a fit of adoration the intelligent girl in love, having nothing to do while he is at work, meticulously describes each painting, its subject matter, not only naming precisely the colors used for each, but much more, his manner of going about it, chock full of the particulars that a woman with the powers of observation of a Sherlock Holmes might write down in a delirious longhand of love. The book will be published next year by Station Hill Press, as soon as the paintings themselves can be located.

Delicate duplicate imprints that puncture the smooth brilliant skin of a poisonous orange toadstool are made by the toenails of a tiny poisonous toad the same color—so that when the toad sits on the toadstool it is invisible, except for two shiny beads that are its big gray eyes, appearing to be just two warts on the toadstool.

Ancient stunted trees on cliffs display their whorls and gnarls to a naturalist who lisps.

He makes a turban out of a patchwork quilt and wears a bullet-proof vest in order to walk without injury into a Texas hailstorm.

His toes sticking out of his sandals are the only vulnerable targets for the walnut-sized hailstones, but soon he has four broken toes—on each foot—and he stumbles in pain, falls to the ground, and finds it impossible to reach the other side of his backyard to save the chickens from certain death.

Eight men are singing like a barbershop quartet at the head of a casket that holds a corpse dressed in red, in exactly the same costume that each singer wears. They are the baseball club of a brewery. The third baseman's dead.

He is pugnacious, portly and a pretender, a pathological liar. He claims that in his youth he'd been a boxer, and lies about his losses as another might brag about his victories. He never says he wins the bouts—always he loses—but he'd gone ten rounds with so-and-so, and lost on a technical knockout; or he'll modestly say he hadn't done too well—been knocked cold in three rounds—when he had fought the champion, and he lives on on the glamor in the tavern.

A baby raccoon and its mother scamper across the tin roof of a summer cottage, and leap into a treetop. Below, a four-year-old boy scampers across the room and grabs a potato from a bag on the floor beside the refrigerator, and with all his might throws the potato at the slanting tin ceiling, making a banging noise, and then he runs to his sleeping mother's bed, and climbs in.

The view of the oncoming storm is especially splendid and dramatic for the electrical worker atop the high-voltage tower that is perched on the edge of the Grand Canyon, overlooking a double bending of the ever-wending Colorado River.

A fast talker sometimes needs to whisper. She is a deaf-mute who can read his lips, is expert at taking shorthand, and gets it all down in black and white, though she's a dozen feet away, and looking at him in a mirror.

Black-eyed Susans fill a field beside a sandy road that twists down an incline through a riverbed of ferns and white poplars, where an eagle sits upon a stump, and six crows walk about the ground around the carcass of a 12-point buck with a bullet through its heart. A faraway barking of a dog is fading out.

Collecting stones of different sizes on the blazing Beach of Sighs the stonemason collects blank tombstones in an orange wheelbarrow.

The especially sweet giant banana grows only on the uninhabited Duke of Gloucester Islands in the South Pacific. A shipwrecked ship's cook finds fresh water on the largest of those islands and survives eating coconuts, bananas and birds, while successfully catching fish with a net in the surf. He is an unlikely gourmet with an inventive mind, so with much time on his hands and many bananas he begins to remove and collect the unusually long and thick strings that grow between the skin and the flesh of the banana, but which are strangely unattached to either. He learns to lay the giant sticky strings out on broken coconut shells to bake in the sun. The gourmet has never tasted anything quite so good. The wonderful food on the island is amazingly varied and easily attainable, and each dish he cooks is seasoned with a mush of sticky strings, often in a silvery sauce, and he daydreams of introducing these dishes to the world in a restaurant in Paris. But he stays there for years refining his recipes—growing into perfect health—and though he is never rescued, though he never leaves the island, nor sees another human being, he knows—this unlikely gourmet on a godforsaken island—that he is the happiest man on earth.

While conglomerates congeal, the Modern Poetry Corporation diversifies.

1932
& 4 untitled paragraphs

I bought a secondhand Studebaker convertible from a used-car dealer in Pittsburgh in 1932 when nothing cost very much and nobody had any money. Not having a job, I spent most of my time in the garage behind the house, working on the car and keeping it in tip-top condition with numberless applications of polish. One afternoon the motor gave out, but I could never afford to get it repaired. When I moved, I left the car in the garage. I'd kept it polished, and except for the motor, the shining car was in tip-top condition.

A steamshovel parks all night in front of my house. And now a giant crane blocks the driveway, and a revolving cement mixer blocks traffic on the street, while between the two a piledriver throws its shadow across my studio window—it's all entertainment for my neighbor's three-year-old grandchild, visiting today from out of town.

To advertise their stamina and sturdiness, the Grand Prix of drag-racing electric automobiles takes place up and down the foothills of the Himalayas on the muddy mountain slopes of India during the monsoon, when those roads become rivers of mud, when electric fish fill rivers, indeed—and where the great night race can be viewed in the distance under natural light as the mountain valley fills with incessant electrical storms.

On an empty seat beside me on a bus I find an obviously expensive pair of gloves that are too small for me, a tag on one of them bearing queer words in an unfamiliar alphabet indicating that they are probably of foreign manufacture. And they've been purchased recently, I sense, in a far-off foreign land.

In slamming on its brakes to avoid hitting a tiny silver roadster with Jersey licence plates, the twenty-ton yellow tractor-trailer truck jackknifes—exploding halfway through the Holland Tunnel, causing a leak that is unpluggable, so that in a matter of an hour the tunnel fills with water from shore to shore.

Ali Baba & the 40 Whisperers
& 4 untitled paragraphs

It is a quiet kind of choir. They call themselves "The 40 Whisperers." The group consists of twenty married couples. The conductor takes the name of "Ali Baba." He trains them to whisper in unison, *without moving their lips.* They carefully spread themselves out among the audience, pretending to be part of the audience. They then perform stories of the Arabian Nights, 40 people whispering the words in unison, Ali Baba standing at the center of the stage, wearing a turban and pantaloons, moving his arms in the manner of a choirmaster, as if the whole audience were his choir. The choirmembers, pretending to be audience, look around to the right and to the left, as if trying to determine where the whispering is coming from, those whispered words that come from everywhere.

I hear a sour note that makes me shiver—like a squawk of a crow in falsetto—and then I see the squawker, a small iridescent bird, land on a shining railroad track reflecting sunlight, now joined by her mate so brilliant yellow he seems to be made of metallic gold, and with shivering whining notes they sing a staccato duet like a zither, that by its beauty makes me shudder.

There is a breed of rabbit which can subsist on playing-cards...which live in top hats of magicians...which can be taught to wink one eye when stared at...which can carry on a conversation with a dummy (that one that travels with the ventriloquist).

At 4 a.m. there is not a whisper of a breeze, while surreptitiously and silently the hammers in the dark do their work—removing nails—so that this foul and dreadful eyesore will fall apart with a loud and dreadful crash to be heard three blocks away when a breeze picks up at dawn.

A skunk at midnight in moonlight is luminous to us behind a maple, a gorgeous tail afloat behind it as it wobbles along a forest pathway, bobbing about in moon shadows, the undulating bright white line along its back stark in the dark.

The Giant Cigar
& 4 untitled paragraphs

It's a giant cigar that's meant to be shared on a bicycle built for two one-legged acrobats as they ride the bike on a singular circular circus tightrope one hundred feet above the center ring, sharing a cigar without a net.

From within gray silhouettes on Scottish islands come scary screams of seabirds calling sailing invisible through the fog that hugs the craggy morning shorelines.

In a Michigan marsh a new kind of cattail appears, different parts of the plant becoming different intensities of saffron yellow. It is a superweed that takes over the marsh, forcing out half the species which have grown here, and growing out yellowy in places where the other half have been, so that many square miles of marsh and borders of streams that mingle in it become totally—and for the entire year—endlessly changing shades of yellow, except for the purple patches of violets and loosestrife.

A tropical setting of postcard quality of palm tree and beach of white sand with afternoon rain that is a relief every day from everyday heat, and which puts lightning and thunder—and more—on the tourist's agenda, for a waterspout can be seen approaching their small boat, where they sip drinks on deck; soon it might be raining small fish, and more.

In sunlight as a mote, a mile-high condor floats and so can see on a canyon's flat floor a fallen mountain goat.

I Sold My Stomach to a Surgeon
& 5 untitled paragraphs

I sold my stomach to a surgeon who, at my death, will give it to a stranger, and in such operations, says the surgeon, the donor must have a strong stomach.

Insistently shaking a bunch of baby rattles, the troublemaker wears a jade green jumpsuit covered with emerald costume jewelry and a Mickey Mouse mask with a scarlet Fu Manchu moustache—she carries an empty cage with its door swinging open, and loudly proclaims that she has lost a rare Irish rattlesnake.

He trips on the doorsill and falls into a room onto a rug and the rug slips out from under him so that his feet fly up into the air and his head hits the corner of an umbrella stand which spews out four umbrellas across the linoleum floor.

A piano mover steals a gargoyle from the roof of a Russian Orthodox church in Paris and sells it to an American piano manufacturer whom he's met at a sidewalk cafe, where they'd begun to talk about pianos while drinking Pernod, and then one thing just leads to another.

Words on the page, words being spoken, words whispered, words in code, words in a foreign language, words that can be understood by a pet, words written phonetically, words oh etcetera!—well, yes...but if we might throw out mystic words that flash back aboriginal signals out of the Australian outback we might observe more kangaroos on Manhattan sidestreets, more wallabies on Wall Sreet, more platypuses in city parks slinking from our drinking fountains, more kookaburras land on fire escapes at dawn, singing *When It's Sunset in Australia*....

A plastic surgeon covers the oddly-shaped scar on her patient's face with a fine, flat star ruby that a jeweller has had cut into an identical odd shape—but slightly smaller—so that the elegant, delicate stone is perfectly framed by the scar, and glows with the intensity of a moonstone, but red, the color of the moon during an eclipse, while it spookily exhibits its two ruby stars.

The Great Gondola
& 3 untitled paragraphs

The Great Gondola is a gambling ship operating off the coast of Venice in international waters of the Adriatic, catering to tourists who are brought to the fancy, modern ship by a myriad of small gondolas that act as the taxis of Venice, that tax the ingenuity of Venetian police, those colorful carabinieri of the canals.

The big baby animals event of Shanghai is a double Contest of Cuteness consisting in this case of a child with a pet, and they are judged as a pair, the epitomes of cuteness, the winners receiving a royal reception hosted by a Shanghai movie star on national television, the animal and child becoming the leads in a documentary of a delightful two-month tour of the zoos of China.

The beautiful duckling grows into an angry, ugly, overweight swan who on blustery, windy, rainy days lords it over the other swans swimming on the dancing waters of Swan Lake.

Snowflakes flashing by a window of a car parked momentarily during a sudden blizzard pile up in cushions on bushes, transforming a hedge by the bridge into a white wall of snow, so that when after several minutes the snow clouds fly away and the sun reappears, the driver is so blinded by brilliant light reflected off the wall of snow, he drives straight into a shallow river, thereby avoiding a collision with an onrushing express train consisting of a string of eighty-five freight cars that will take five minutes to pass by the dangerous intersection.

The OMD
& 4 untitled paragraphs

The Organization of Midwestern Dentists develops a rifle and pistol as well as a rapid-fire machine gun which sends a succession of two-inch bubbles streaming out twenty yards in a straight line. Inside each bubble is a gigglesworth of laughing gas, furnished by tanks attached to the weapons, tanks which are regularly utilized by members of the OMD, an organization of middle-aged men who indulge for fun in mock military maneuvers and battles. On weekends they dress up in camouflage costumes and run through the woods.

Scratching her tattoo with a chopstick the Pacific Islander with withered skin, a toothless great-great-grandmother, refuses to eat the rice and beans on her palmleaf plate with an angry glance at the brain on top of it of her old friend from a neighboring tribe, whose body has been brought back by her victorious clansmen.

The French ghost is a Sunday painter, who during her lifetime was a champion ice skater—but now wearing rubber-wheeled roller skates, the ghost skates backward silently through halls of The Louvre in the small hours of the night, through centuries of art, dodging guards, skating in circles around freestanding sculptures, vanishing at certain moments....

A writer with a butterfly net embarks at sunset on a nightlong meander through a forest in search of a luna moth. The luna moth embarks at sunset on a nightlong meander through the forest in search of a mate.

Hooray! Hey-Hey! Ho-Ho!—are the first words learned by a laughing bonobo chimpanzee who has been taught to sing by the seven-year-old daughter of an African chieftain, who likes to listen to her father's record collection of English popular music, so that these first words of the chimpanzee are spoken dropping the h's with a Cockney accent.

The Glee of Ghouls
& 7 untitled paragraphs

With the glee of ghouls a costume of the Clown of the Grotesque awaits the Mardi Gras in a box, and every once in a while shakes its bells in anticipation, with the impatience of the beautiful.

Ancient chain. Unbounded mounds of earth dotted by abandoned factory buildings in oily ponds of muddy yellow water, with a wink in the motionless landscape of what might have been the movement of a rat in a shadow.

A Toronto storyteller travels about Canada performing in libraries in numerous small towns, telling tales of the big city to country kids; in libraries of larger cities he tells stories about farm animals; and once a year he returns to Toronto in February for the Storytellers' Convention, telling an audience of storytellers his tales of dragonflies, talking frogs and fairies who live underwater.

A small cast-iron statue falls to the floor off the mantle near a big bay window in a new San Francisco residence. It isn't the great earthquake, but is a minor precursor that nevertheless has its say, a mumbled word spoken with a rumble that makes the houses sway, but no one in the nineteenth century understands the word.

"Six hundred and sixty!" quickly answers a quick-witted, elegant and elderly plumber, wearing a tuxedo and holding a holiday champagne glass, happily speaking to his wife at a party celebrating their Diamond Anniversary—when she asks, "During sixty years of working on tubs and sinks, how many diamonds down drains have you rescued?"

Down does a waterlogged lifeboat fall beneath the swell of the churning surface into calmer waters abounding with fish-eating fish, into purple regions below the sunlight and on down into darker dungeons of the depths where darting luminosities develop and diving whales descend, down it goes, a lifeboat containing twelve corpses dead of starvation and of drinking salt water, whose only survivor, the thirteenth, now is drinking chicken soup on the deck of the rescuing racing yacht, that famous American boat which will lose the neck-and-neck race by a nose, by a length—by a length of time no longer than it takes to read this paragraph.

Running through the woods down a single railroad track which no train has been down for years, a sneaker landing on each third tie, the nine-year-old dodges to the right and left to avoid the giant goldenrod that grow between the rails, and he's gotten halfway to his destination (a swimming lake) when he stumbles to a stop...for ten feet away and what would be directly in front of an onrushing train there stands a cow...wow!

The dog that reminds me of my uncle bites him when he meets him.

Swimming Squirrels
& 7 untitled paragraphs

During the month of May the patterns of fallen seeds and petals on the surface of the heated swimming pool are disturbed by several swimming squirrels, which make paths that criss-cross through the lovely litter.

The shoulder of a boulder becomes the border of a corner-stone (the center of a ceremony) of a great new building onto which words are carved with the same chisel and by the same hand of the same man who will carve the words onto the architect's tombstone.

From the treasure chest he takes a roll of gold coins wrapped in llama-skin vellum—from the roll the pirate takes a coin and with a single stroke of a hatchet cuts the coin in half, and in obvious awe, asks his peg-legged shipmate, "Can I shave with it? What will you take for it, the hatchet?"

The gambler gobbles appetizers, a night club singer takes a snort of snuff, a chef does a dance holding a frying pan in each hand, while a waitress changes into her uniform and a door-man examines his moustache in the mirror, and a bouncer squeezes a rubber ball in an absent-minded exercise, the owner, himself, speaks out loud in a hoarse voice, to nobody, "It's time to get down to business."

A rich little girl inherits from her multi-millionaire grandfa-ther a collection of sabers and swords, and her other, poor grand-father, who has been a circus worker all his life, teaches her the art of swallowing them.

He breeds mockingbirds in brilliant colors, each worth its weight in gold, for each produces a poison in a gland behind its beak that can kill any bird it pecks at, but can also cure many depressed persons of their symptoms, as can their songs, some-times.

We workers at the wholesale jewelry firm shovel gemstones with teaspoons into muffin tins, distinguishing quality, color and size, and use tablespoons to ladle pearls and turquoise spheres the size of huckleberries.

An unexpected avalanche, a rockslide on Mount Fuji, leaves many boulders balanced one atop another at its base, the balanced stones in a line like an art exhibit by the god of sculpture.

Many Balanced Boulders
& 3 untitled paragraphs

On the last day of summer camp downstream from their camp-site in a riverbed of boulders a hundred Boy Scouts become possessed by an idea for that final afternoon and with unbounded energy they begin to balance pairs of boulders one atop the other until they have a Boulder Show that they will never forget, a vivid vista of hundreds of pairs of balanced boulders bathed in evening sunlight—casting long shadows—a bright yellow vision to be invoked in their old age in a golden blink of total recall.

A gypsy tailor down the block has a faraway look in his eyes—as if he is seeing the future—as he presses my father's suit while I wait for it, sitting on a wooden bench.

A good-looking guy gets a spot on his tie as he is about to go out to a ballgame with his girl, and so he cuts a piece of clothes-line the appropriate length, inserts it into his collar and ties it into a Windsor knot, just as he would tie his necktie, and his girl thinks it looks swell; so later that evening when they attend a dress-up, black-tie ball, he wears the same thing—he paints the clothesline black with India ink—and he starts a fashion.

He chimes in singing as he chortles, as he sings he can't stop laughing—it's what is called a joyous melody.

I Do Like To Trawl
& 5 untitled paragraphs

He says in a Southern accent, "Yankees like to fish with tridents, but I do like to trawl."

"It's a hip and a hop for a scallop from the grasshopper shop to the jump rope store of the rabbit," says the miniature kangaroo.

A dandelion inspires the wrath of a lawn owner who angrily grabs a spade and lunges at the yellow blossom, but misses and hits a rock buried just beneath the soil so that the tool bends out of his hand, and his knuckles strike the stone and begin to bleed and swell, causing the man to yelp and swear and stamp the earth in rage, aiming with his heel at the poor plant, but his upraised leg stops in midair, and poised in pain, he shrieks in bewilderment with a pulled hamstring and a wrenched calf muscle, so that finally he faints, falling to the ground unconscious in silent writhing misery.

Closed because of death in the Family says a sign on a door of the shoemaker's shop on the day I need my shoes for the marathon dance contest.

Waggle & Wiggle—the Wag and the Wig—were an English comedy team well known in America at the end of the nineteenth century, where they toured for thirty years on the vaudeville circuits. They finally quit in San Francisco, where, in fact, they had been born, for they were frauds as Englishmen, though, as artists, genuine.

A sampan is loaded with chocolate for China, and is raided by pirates in the China Sea, who find the unfamiliar cargo rather queer, and disappointing. They throw the chocolate overboard, and steal the boat. Down below, the packages are torn apart and devoured by sharks.

Eight at the Gate
& 4 untitled paragraphs

There are eight at the gate who all want dinner! And so I tell them we could serve them broiled cumin, with roasted basil and boiled peppercorns, and frozen powdered curry for dessert. And now each holds a fork and a spoon in each fist, and that is them, pounding on the table impatiently—demanding dinner!

A laughing lady counts the spots on the ladybug's back.

Halfway there we stop for lunch between the bridges on an island in a restaurant called Midway Manor where the meal is not half bad.

We breed albinos with black teeth.

Imagine salad falls onto this page, these words obscured by opaque ketchup, and now I imagine the sudden red thought of a reader.

Her Doll Looks Disturbed
& 2 untitled paragraphs

Her doll looks disturbed, her giraffe is grim, her teddy bear truculent, her porcelain pony is legless, her stuffed dog is snarling, and her toy rattlesnake bares its fangs in a crazy smile. It is the toystore lady's collection of things she couldn't sell.

It takes the cake—a salad fork stuck into an orange—and wins First Prize in a color photography contest, the picture purchased for a large sum by the Silver Company, whose elegant fork is made famous by the funny photo.

I am standing at the pinnacle, and report that the pinnacle does not end in a point...when one gets to the top one encounters a valley.

The Pampered Muscular Alaskan
& 16 untitled paragraphs

The pampered muscular Alaskan whose parents are sled dogs is acquired as a puppy by a ski resort in New Hampshire, is soon adopted as its mascot and is doted on by everyone and is the delight of their tame moose.

They started a fashion throughout the country among pre-highschool girls. An eighth grader finds a bunch of bustles in her great-grandmother's attic as well as the silk dresses custom-made to accommodate them—and she and half-a-dozen chums wear them at their eighth-grade graduation dance.

A picket fence turns to meet a trellis with which it shares white roses.

At the source of the Blue Nile a crimson banjo floats down a slow Ethiopian stream beside an overturned canoe and a green paddle.

Names of places, names of faces grace old coins in buried boxes.

To the delight of a happy, laughing crowd of cartoonists their host fills a punchhowl with punchlines, and furnishing them with ink and pens and paper, he holds a cartoon contest, and the cartoonists themselves in a vote choose the winner, with the only stipulation that they not vote for themselves, the winner receiving a well-paying assignment to do a book of cartoons on a year-long expedition into the interior of Antarctica.

She is a big-boned girl with fallen arches who grows seven feet tall by the time she is twelve, and she is terrified of setting foot on a rope-and-wood suspension bridge outside her home town in Chile, necessary whenever her school basketball team plays their archrivals over in a neighboring village on the other side of the canyon.

A youngster and an oldster walk along a boardwalk, one skipping lightly along and the other limping and lagging behind, setting the pace of the pair. The doctor that put the boy's foot in a cast, tells the boy's grandfather that the result of the old man's biopsy is negative.

He turns over in bed in the middle of the night and sees brilliant flashing lights thrown on his ceiling from outside his bedroom window and hears the shouting voice of a fireman and a neighbor scream. When he closes his eyes the voices vanish. When he opens them, he awakes from a dream into daylight, and hears his neighbor scream—at her children, as usual—making the usual noise.

He invests his time and wastes his money on making expeditions onto four continents amassing a most complete collection of queer and deadly quicksands, and he bequeaths these costly viscous patches of earth to the Los Angeles Museum of Natural History, which builds a room with his money to exhibit them to throngs, indeed—to *hordes* of avid schoolchildren.

Once more at the Laundromat, gathering in wooly waters, socks and sweaters spin again.

On the Fourth of July, Christmas decorations and peppermint candy canes cover a ten-foot dried-out Christmas tree that has completely dropped its needles, blanketing unopened presents that six months ago had been carefully placed beneath the tree.

The noisy brook becomes a quiet stream on down a gentle incline, and soon the stream settles into a swamp and loses itself in shallow pools which spread among small tufted islands of soggy turf and slender trees.

A verticality of palm trees adorns the horizon of a low Carribean island, uninhabited except for crabs and turtles scooting through the surf, but abounding with big white birds, and harboring a family of feral domestic cats, which subsists entirely on small lizards ard sandpipers, there being on the island no rats, snakes or people.

He holds a cut-glass goblet to her nose, and then to her ear, so that she might smell, and then hear the viscous mysterious mixture of birch bark resins bubbling goldenly in slow motion—and as honey does, smelling of an insect—golden globes slowly rising, shining yellow pearls that vanish at the surface with a pleasant popping, peppering piquantly a careful listener's eardrum.

Copperplate etchings clutter his tables that, themselves, clutter the etcher's studio, while discarded etchings are lying all over the floor—but the place should be seen on Sunday morning when he's finished reading *The Times.*

A poor soccer team on tour runs out of money on the road when their bus runs out of gas, and their boss runs out on them, leaving them stranded between two towns in Iowa, which later when they try to tell people about it, they are unable to find on any map.

The Green Mechanic
& 3 untitled paragraphs

The green mechanic takes a wrench from a tool bench, puts it in his pocket and walks across a hangar to where a small airplane sits with its motor exposed and with several of its parts lying on a cloth on the ground awaiting their insertion into the machine. With the wrench the novice removes a nut from a bolt, and for a half an hour he putters around cleaning and replacing all the parts until the motor is finished, ready to roar. He closes a casing over the motor and locks it, and then notices a nut and bolt—obviously belonging in the machine—still lying on the dropcloth. He tries the motor and the exhaust is bright green. He sighs, and his breath is bright green.

Under a spreading maple he sits down on a large stone, and he examines a fragile pebble that breaks apart on pressure being applied by his thumb, and inside it he finds a fossil of a maple seed, hard as a rock.

An octopus emerges from the surf and runs down the beach in moonlight...in broad daylight on the following day a good-sized octopus emerges from the surf and runs along the edge of the water chasing a beachball.

All sorts of sailboats and motorized launches surround the Royal Yacht that carries the Queen into the Caribbean port for a ceremony which will give the island its independance. Later that morning in a slow amble through the center of town the Queen, accompanied by the mayor's wife and several of the Queen's companions, stop to shop at several stores—and the weather has put her into a good mood. "I feel like having fun," she says. They stand in a large store that sells tropical birds, and she asks its owner if he will sell every bird in the shop. He agrees, he is given a check, and all the birds are set free. "With the understanding" she says, "that you will not close your shop today, that you will not close the cages of the birds that are free, and that you'll put food in their cages for them to eat should they return. It must be further understood that any birds who return are yours, and that birds who do not return are a gift from me to the city." So that now—at this moment, on this day of all days—trees in the park in the center of town are filled with rare and beautiful birds.

The Tip of the Nose
& 6 untitled paragraphs

Using a silencer on his high-powered rifle, a sharpshooter within a week removes the tip of the nose of every statue in the city, and then in the befuddlement of his strange rage, he cuts off his own nose for spite.

She wears a straw hat with a green ribbon, and I wear a black straw hat with a typewriter ribbon.

Austere moonflowers that bloom in dim light after dark have dignities daisies lack—they do not hang their heads nor do they wag them about in the breeze.

To finance botanical expeditions into Brazilian jungles, a huge tropical greenhouse in Toronto takes the profits from an elegant restaurant situated at the center of the greenhouse, where fresh tropical fruit and unusual Amazonian vegetables are served during blizzards and ice storms to that part of the population which will pay to be warm, in a place abounding in cold winter days and nasty nights. In the evening they serve South American cuisine and feature a Brazilian dance band.

An ambulance races down an icy street in the freezing small hours of the morning returning in a life-and-death rush to the hospital emergency room, its siren resounding and blending in with the long whistle of the midnight train (late again!).

Though a pocket full of gold coins jingles just like silver, the weight upon the thigh bespeaks a mystery that coins of silver lack.

A gorgeous cat walks along a wooden fence and leaps down onto the roof of a doghouse. Inside it a coyote sleeps. The cat has come back for the first time in a week and finds nobody here. In the backyard there are a dozen mounds he's never seen before, and there is a tunnel entrance beside each little hill—prarie dogs have taken over. During his absence the lawn has turned brown. Deer have entered an open gate and eaten everything in the garden. There is no way the cat can get into the house. Inside, the telephone begins to ring, but after a while the caller hangs up.

To Ulag-Ijiji
& 8 untitled paragraphs

Because he loves the rain he moves his large family and extensive furnishings to Ulag-Ijiji, a small island that has a greater annual rainfall rate than any other place on earth. Soon warp and rot destroy the furniture, each of his family becomes infected by a different disfiguring, life-threatening tropical disease, and because of an irregularity in the island's small bank, their life savings are lost, and they become destitute. After a number of years a distant relative appears with an umbrella on their dilapidated doorstep, and offers to pay the family's way back to Connecticut, but the offer is rejected—so soothing is the endless rain, so conducive to everyone's peace of mind that the idea of returning to the United States seems just as outlandish to them...as they seem outlandish to us.

Below a mulberry tree grows a blackberry bush, and below the bush is a patch of huckleberries. Quietly eating, a child hears a chipmunk sneeze.

A fallen tree holds out a broken branch that holds up a blue jay's nest, amazingly still right side up, at eye level, containing three vociferous juvenille birds, their noisemaking wavering between quavering squeaks and raucous squawks, only interrupted by wriggling worms dropped into gaping mouths by the father blue jay.

On center court—in a final match—a Texas Women's Tennis Champion is challenged by an upstart wearing purple polka-dot pants and by bad luck, for in a sudden storm she is knocked out cold by hail the size of tennis balls, and as a tornado touches down many in the audience are injured as the wooden stands collapse, as also does the referee.

After numerous washings it will take all Summer in the sun to completely dry out—soggy upholstery from the Summer Palace found after the Yellow River flood, soaked in yellow mud.

A television seminar of the most famous dummies, half a dozen of them sitting with their silent partners (six ventriloquists) discussing actual personal lives of the most well-known talkshow hosts, well-researched ugly gossip of a sort that can make not only eyebrows rise, but hair stand on end, make husbands leave wives...and turn professional comedians into laughingstocks.

The tiniest mammal turns out to be a fruit bat, previously considered, because of its very small size, to be the common fruit gnat.

A mingling of matadors in full costume in a tavern adjacent to the great bullring in Madrid, the most active of the many in Spain, has led to many fistfights and to roughhouse wrestling on the sawdust floor, so that the costumes of silver and silk soon become tarnished and ripped, and dripped on and stained by the best purple port in the world.

Brandishing an ancient weapon, a night watchman at the Tibetan Museum, ordinarily unarmed on his rounds through the night, hears unexpected noises and so grabs the nearest weapon from a wall, a spear sprouting barbs and razor-sharp multiple tips, and feels first brave, but foolhardy—and finally foolish on finding three mice cavorting among the Buddhist bells.

Where the Yukon Meets the Klondike
& 2 untitled paragraphs

Where the Yukon meets the Klondike—down Dawson way—sled dogs of prospectors are often afflicted by cavities, and a local dentist fills all their teeth with gold.

He whistles a tune without making a sound and silently snaps his fingers in time to the tune.

Once again she doubles her bet. Players and lookers-on murmur and mumble and notice—she herself seems the only person not to realize it—that the croupier who spins the wheel is her double.

A Panic of Pit Bulls
& 5 untitled paragraphs

In a panic of pit bulls pandemonium predominates when a full-grown, muscular Siamese tomcat scratches three noses in quick succession while belting out a fearful feline shriek, a horrifying screech that can terrify, as only a cat can, so that three dogs with bloody noses fall over one another, loudly scratching the cement with their toenails, scrambling in terror to escape, for each had got a shot of the Adrenaline of Dread—in the nose.

A silver salver of caviar of swordfish to be spread on a sliver of coconut is not her regular breakfast, but she finds it delicious as doughnuts, while eating a toasted wrasse and sipping a glass of passionfruit juice.

A large and perfect carrot sprouting luxuriant deep green leaves wins the Beautiful Vegetable contest at the Arkansas State Fair, beating a beauteous beet that looks like a peach, a spherical head of orange lettuce and a giant potato...and here honorable mention must be made for "the most wonderful pun" in the award-name *Best of the Fair.*

An angler dangles his ankles in the cool stream under a hot, blue sky and a gibbous moon, as a buzzing in the bushes and a birdsong from some rushes inspires him to speak aloud a rhymey poem, doggerel he's memorized as a child.

A deposed king of great wealth gets to Texas where he then builds a palace, and there gives great parties and old-world-style balls—in the palace in place of his old major-domo, who is lame and can't speak English, he hires away from a Texas football team a beautiful drum majorette to superintend the fashionable affairs in his new home, and to his delight, an expert at twirling the major-domo's baton.

The turtle paddles upon a pond staring up at a crisp crescent moon in the deep blue sky, its neck stretched out into the air, and then it dives down and swims along the gravel bottom among the fixtures of the fish, among those uncanny pairs of stones, one balanced on the other, that sit in the sand like underwater furniture—the whole scene being the set for a Lincoln Center dance concert in which my reader takes the lead and dances the part of the turtle, the author being your audience.

The Dinosaur's Big Toe
& an untitled paragraph

A fossil of a late Cretaceous dinosaur's big toe stands out at the top of an orange rock, and astonishingly balanced on the perfectly formed toenail of the monster is another boulder of a somewhat later time, from the Tertiary Period. At the lower extremity of the second rock is a fossil of a small mammal, which stands on one foot balanced like a ballet dancer on the tip of the giant toenail. The two rocks rest in a cave protected from the changing winds of the Gobi Desert, and are discovered at the same moment and examined closely by two colleagues, archeologists, one of Beijing University, one from Harvard. The two rocks are carefully removed and they are brought back by the scientists to the Chinese university, where they now can be seen balanced at the entrance to the walled garden of the Archeology Department, under an Oriental arch, protected from the changing winds and the rain of Beijing.

We're here together, my goat and I, all set to climb the slope on which I had rescued him two years ago when he was just a kid, when his mother had been killed in an avalanche. But now no amount of coaxing will convince him to accompany me upward. He whimpers miserably. My mountain goat is afraid of heights.

Songs of Butterflies
& 9 untitled paragraphs

The ultrasonic songs of sunlit butterflies in flight can be heard a hundred yards away in the dark by bats as they hang asleep, who twitch at that faraway sound while they dream.

The curious wife of a sleeping thief, who has earlier stolen eight doughnuts for her from a burgled flat, finds his sticky pockets chock-full of crumbs and emeralds.

A circus midget retires to Ireland where he acquires an Irish Wolfhound which he rides like a horse, using a saddle and stirrups which have been custom-made to fit the two of them. The dog has shoes that make a sound when he runs over cobblestones or pavement—but often not quite like a galloping horse—for he's been taught to be a trotter.

Lost, but about to discover *A Place of Long-legged Birds,* a minor wilderness of the remote Adirondacks—sliding down a wet hillside in softly falling rain, grasping plants and branches of small trees to keep from careening downward with a rush on slippery greenery, a descending party of explorers, half a dozen twelve-year-olds in Boy Scout uniforms are seeking a beautiful place to go swimming that they have heard about, and though they are lost, they will soon discover it, the same place that 500 years ago indigenous Indians had also named *A Valley of Pools* in a language not spoken for centuries.

A hotshot with a slingshot turns twelve on New Year's Eve and goes amok with mischief-making, organizing a window-breaking contest among his friends during the last single hour of an old year, a celebration of his childhood's final hour.

A robin swallows a centipede that has just eaten a thorn on a Jimsonweed. The centipede is immune to the poison of the thorn, but not the robin, who immediately vomits and dies, his body decimated by twenty centipedes.

The streetlamps on this smalltown road have been installed at different times and are in different styles. Several are fog-piercing yellow sodium lamps, two are bluish, others greenish, though pinker and plainer whites predominate. I call my white dog *Chameleon,* for each evening when we take our walk she keeps changing color.

Giant mosquitoes careen between sunlit Japanese lanterns at a lakeside cafe while dragonflies dance at the water's edge—the bumblebees drink beer from dregs of mugs and flies climb down outsides of straws in emptied glasses, and while the lazy waitress sits reading my book, several customers are trying to attract her attention without success.

Each iceberg is mounted by Spaniards and driven by a mysterious means as an armada of melting icebergs moves south, soon fills the Irish Sea chock-full and jams and chills the English Channel so that harbors and bays of British ports freeze over, and Spanish revenge is finally attained on the English weather, which in another century had destroyed the other armada.

During a thunderstorm a marble-sized meteorite crashs through a skylight and buries itself in the skull of a stuffed deer so that its antlers each break off and fall with a rattling clatter onto a wet red marble floor on sparkling shards of skylight glass, while the meteorite itself becomes a smoking lump in the throat of the deer.

A Somewhat Secret Assignation
& an untitled paragraph

The cardboard toboggan is a corrugated box the size of a refrigerator that is flattened and sat on by three girls who fly down a snow-covered hillside with such momentum that they slide out onto a sidewalk on the edge of the park incredibly plowing into their fifth-grade homeroom teacher who just happens to be passing on a somewhat secret assignation with their school's new principal.

In an Australian circus six koalas do a complicated trapeze and high-wire act in the center ring, and for doing their tricks, the trainer rewards them with eucalyptus-flavored cough drops.

During The Dayslong Rainstorm
& 10 untitled paragraphs

During a dayslong rainstorm a dozen barges in drydock are set afloat and set free in the middle of the night by suddenly rising floodwaters of the Ohio River. Two days later when the waters recede, the whole bunch are discovered still together five miles downstream, half a mile from the river, filling a parking lot and blocking the access to a shopping mall.

I turn a radio off. Through a wall I hear my neighbor's radio turned to the same station, and rather loud. Someone turns it off, and I become aware of the same program from yet another radio coming through a different wall, from an apartment of another neighbor on the other side. Then that sound ceases, and there is silence. It was really a bad program.

Fog on a pond is whispy and warm, from translucent to dense at the dock, becoming opaque at one end of a black pool which wanders off like a river for a mile—but one that does not run—for in fact it is a narrow, curling lake of black mud surrounded by the five-foot ferns of a bog through which a dinghy can be poled from one end to the other without our being able to see a shoreline, yet we are never farther than twenty feet from the shore. For the whole of our trip we are accompanied by an invisible songbird who seems to be able to see us, for it stays just behind us, singing away all the time.

A young boy twists around and frowns and is reluctant to have his fortune told. When finally he is talked into holding out his palm, it is seen to contain a Mexican jumping bean.

Though reasonable, some things are unimaginable. A girl in a helicopter five hundred feet up in the air drops a tennis ball that lands on a tennis court, but instead of bouncing, it bursts, making a sound like a ringing of a rubber bell.

Below a tree line near a top of a mountain a forest fire is started by a single midnight lightning stroke, which then steals around the mountainside in both directions, becoming a circle of fire around the mountaintop, the red circle of flames seen between rainclouds by passengers flying the red-eye from San Francisco to New York City.

Foghorns of tugboats boop long in unison in the middle of a sunny Sunday as a weighted body of a revered old tugboat captain slides along a plank from beneath an Irish flag and drops into the deepest part of New York Harbor in a formal funeral, a burial at sea in the precise place that he had wanted it.

She dips her tiny brush into a mixture of brown and yellow and blue—a bilious green suggestive of excrement and vomit—with which she paints her toenails and fingernails. She laughingly calls it My Ugly Green, that Irish nurse who can make them giggle, and who starts a fashion of adornment among nurses at the Home for the Aged.

A Russian meringue pie made with gold leaf shines like the dome of a Moscow church.

Ripple marks on the sand along an ocean beach a hundred thousand years ago are covered by a foot-thick layer of volcanic ash, and now can be found fossilized in New York City on a counter, where those very ripples can be purchased in that store for thirty-five dollars.

Like a rouged white sponge, a dermatologist has a complexion of a cauliflower dusted with red pepper, while his wife has fine features and bone structure of a beauty, but the skin of a cantalope and crackling voice of an old man.

A Racehorse Put To Pasture
& an untitled paragraph

A racehorse put to pasture after winning many races is a show-off and a beauty to behold as it gallops along an immense wooden fence that encircles a posh pasture, running as if racing, but not unaware of noisy throngs—of songbirds, and the crowds amidst tall grass—of wildflowers.

He sits in sunlight and licks his feathers. His coat is white, his face flat, but instead of fur he has feathers. The cat with feathers can't fly, yet he looks terribly elegant. That cat is named Pomposity, but for short, we call him Polly.

Ringleader of the Gang
& 18 untitled paragraphs

A ringleader of a gang of third-grade girls runs along a top of an eight-foot-tall wooden fence, displaying a remarkable sense of balance as well as fearlessness—and none of her pals, neither boys nor girls, would dare to do it as she does, as if doing nothing more dangerous than dancing along the edge of the gutter.

The wiz of Chinese showbiz opens a twenty-foot Chinese fan to a sound of a bass drum and a brass band and signals the entrance onstage at the United Nations of a hundred acrobats juggling umbrellas, on each of which is written in a different language the phrase *new millennium.*

His hobby is working crossword puzzles, and to help him in this he has a box containing a special set of words which he calls his chatterbox, and much in the manner that poisonous animals sport brilliantly colored bodies the chatterbox is painted with big red dots and green and purple stripes to discourage the curious.

This week a black squirrel scampers happily upon a tree of charcoal which last year had been set afire when hit by lightning in that virgin forest which still exists in the year 2000, pristine in the State of Maine, that whole state which this week is covered by a record-breaking snowfall.

He could tie complicated knots in the dark and imitate the song of a skylark, yet here he is, adrift and all at sea and lonely in London, sitting on a green bench under a green branch in a fancy English park in the rain without an umbrella, wearing a dirty Irish sweater and—let alone without a shilling—he wears shirt and pants without pockets.

He has a great big boathouse attached to his garage. He puts purple pontoons on a small, dull gray dirigible so that it could land on the surface of the lake near his house, as well as rise into the air from there, and he finds that that is much easier than attaching its nose to a pole.

They should have been in bed asleep, but three children at the top of a four-story stairwell, straddling a brightly varnished and beautifully waxed bannister, slide down it unimpeded from top to bottom, landing on a polar bear rug in a giggling heap.

A 16-point buck turns its head to stare curiously at a splash.

Three sisters run a ranch, where they have a bunch of buffalo. They become sharpshooters with bow and arrow, and are able to get in at least an hour's practice every day, clearing their property of rattlesnakes.

When a thing is impossible to do, it makes it easier not to do it.

A shout of a snowman is bland in greeting the sun in a field of birds each day at dawn compared to the harsh abrupt scream that is the snow-covered scarecrow's squawk, who the birds all know is blind.

He finds a football standing on end in the woods, balanced snugly in a dimple of a half-buried boulder, surrounded by a stand of moss and violets.

He cultivates rotten eggs with strong shells (good for throwing) and a guaranteed stink, and he sells them to politically active people, particularly those with passions to vent at demonstrations. A message conveyed by an old-fashioned rotten egg is eloquent when the target's your tie, and when you have a shell in smithereens across your vest and have, whenever you stop long enough to speak to someone, that odor hover over you.

Atop a cherrypicker on a beach buggie children pick cherrystone clams at Orchard Beach—where seashells grow on trees—there where tree toads sing every evening, then when warm sand hides viscous puddles of tar to be discovered inadvertently by toes and elbows.

The mammoth mound of grain fallen into a shape of a great cone is the responsibility of twelve barn cats who survey and patrol its perimeter from lower wooden beams of a huge old barn that farmhands call Cats Castle.

In a windstorm ripe lemons all fall, rolling in roiling atmosphere down a cultivated hillside, gathering in gullies in large lemon-colored piles, waiting to be gathered into aprons by slightly lemon-colored ladies darkly dressed on a warm and breezy slope in the foothills of the Himalayas in South Nepal.

A fence that surrounds a farmhouse is constructed of white pickets adorned with white rose vines in bloom. The house will be painted navy blue, and rose vines in three quite different shades of red that will cover the whole house are being planted around it in a triple row of vines.

They're temporary contemporaries, each touches an horizon, for as the sun sets in the west in the east a full moon rises—so as we sit in Socrates Park talking, intent on a brief illusion of their hugeness...Lo! the lotus in Deer Park closes, while Socrates keeps talking, or is it the other way around?

When you hear someone humming a tune or whistling to himself, it doesn't mean he loves music—it means he's nervous about something.

The Scarlet Skull and Crossbones
& 17 untitled paragraphs

In an old school building quite early in the morning the old school janitor draws a huge skull and crossbones on a blackboard with a lipstick that has inadvertantly been dropped beneath her desk by a third-grade homeroom teacher, and then with a pail of hot water and a sponge larger than his fist, he spends half an hour removing the greasy scarlet symbol from the expanse of black stone, hastening to finish before the arrival of the children.

One of the last hairy mammoths on earth is gored by a tusk and then abandoned by a trumpeting triumphant elephant. Quickly gathering about the body are a dozen vultures and laughing hyenas, as well as half a dozen laughing women wearing fur coats and bearing choppers made of stone to dismember the beast, and take home the ivory.

The magical high-steel engineer builds bridges of the sort which—with a little forethought—you can cross before you come to them.

The gunsmith constructs a perfectly fiendish water pistol of exquisite workmanship and of exceptional accuracy at ejecting an intensely offensive odorous secretion of a skunk.

After walking five miles to a cabin in the woods, hungry as a dog and consumed by impatience, she can't wait to wolf a porterhouse steak with a portobello mushroom sitting in hot sauce that sits on the cold potbelly stove, and she becomes sick as a dog.

The pugilist squares off with a lamppost after midnight on the way home from the saloon, sparring a few minutes before passing on to the next streetlight, to whom he speaks a few words while giving it a few left jabs, though he does not actually hit the metal post which might result in an injured fist or a bloody knuckle. It is a lovely pantomime in harmless silhouette.

A whole circus tent, all folded up, fits into a tiny room from whence it will be taken in a truck to a train to be transported to Cincinnati, where like a brown moth from its chrysalis it will emerge to spread its wings, and tonight show its colors for all to see under a midwestern moon, illuminated from within by what will seem to be a million electric lightbulbs, while on tenterhooks with troubled looks the joyous gaze at the trapeze.

A gale covers a lawn with walnuts.

They find a dirty domino that is probably covered with salt at the center of a dried-up tropical pond. It is being licked simutaneously by the three funny tongues of a lizard, a hummingbird and a miniature fruit bat. The domino suddenly vanishes—grabbed by a pack rat, who races with it to his nest, where now the domino has become a part of his fantastic collection.

A gingko tree hides among elms that line the block, and on this rainy autumn day all are shedding yellow leaves that splash among the goldenrod.

Your topknot is askew.

There is a marsupial jungle on an isolated island off the North Coast of Australia on which there are no mammals whatsoever, and the Tasmanian tiger reigns as king of the beasts.

Hundreds of mirrors and great sheets of glass stand about a glazier's shop in the middle of the night and as a burglar enters the pitch-black room, the beam of his strong flashlight seeking a safe examines the surrounding walls for a number of minutes, and wherever it touches creates complicated patterns of multiply-reflected light across the storefront window facing Main Street, attracting the attention of a number of passersby, homeward bound from taverns, who are amazed at the kaleidoscopic light show on the window of the darkened store. The goodnatured laughter of that audience of about twenty onlookers is punctuated by an explosion which injures nobody, but instead of opening the safe, the explosive device backfires, shattering at a single moment every sheet of glass and mirror in the store, so that the sound of the explosion itself is completely drowned out by the incredible noise of breaking glass that can be heard a mile away.

A pattern of crimson petunias, vermilion geraniums and scarlet poppies is contrived by the giggling gardener who can't stop laughing at his red thought.

She adroitly catches a moth in her mouth by leaping from the top of a bookcase through the air in the direction of the chandelier.

There is unexpected drama at the theater when a woman in a matinee audience aims a large pistol at an actor who is speaking onstage, and then shouts, "This is real life!" as her pistol explodes, and a bullet pierces the heart of the actor.

When I write, I worry about what things mean, but when I paint, it's just dab...dab...dab...dab....

Two giant gems weigh a quarter of a ton each: Three green sides meet to make three edges that themselves converge where a giant cube of jade balances on its corner in a shallow hollow of a pure ruby boulder—polished to translucent perfection—which in sunlight can cast a scarlet-tinted shadow on the floor of white Italian marble at the feet of a small dark monarch, at the foot of his gold throne in the throne room of his palace, his hereditary home, a small island on a little lake of a tiny Far Eastern kingdom, a pretty pebble plunked down in a crystal puddle among stupendous mountains of prodigious Himalayan enormity.

The Seismographs Jam
& 63 untitled paragraphs

The Tokyo seismographs jam...but in a small and lovely public garden several pairs of balanced boulders topple, and an immediate call reporting it to a radio station—which interrupts a program to report the minor event—gives people in the great city time to remove themselves from danger of collapsing structures from seven earthquakes rated seven which follow within the hour.

In plain sight on a dark day tiny shining drops of drizzle coalescing into brilliant rivulets of light wander down my windowpane.

While walking he is trying to invent a complicated knot, tying various versions in a thick piece of rope, and at the very moment he succeeds, when the idea clicks into completion and the knot assumes its symmetry, he stubs his toe on an orange brick, and breaks a toenail, and in falling, he hurts his arm. It's a kind of happiness.

Near the center of the virgin forest of Maine he finds a brand new bathtub abandoned in the deep woods, sitting in a brook in a foot of water which enters the tub through the drain, filling it to an inch from the top of the tub, the normal amount that one would fill a normal tub, so that it is perfect for taking a bath. Within easy reach of one in the tub, a towel hangs from a nearby branch of a poison sumac tree.

To the detective it appears on first studying the corpse that the young woman's shoes are on the wrong feet, but when the shoes are removed it is revealed that her big toes are on the outside of each foot. And then it is noted that as she lies on her back with the palms of her hands facing downward that her thumbs are on the outside of each hand, as well.

In a back room at the Numismatic Association Convention a dozen coin collectors are shooting craps using olden dice from Biblical times, and using ancient coins for money (and they each know what each of the exotic coins is worth) as they bet against each other on the rolling of the ancient cubes.

This afternoon a gibbous moon looks down upon a troop of baboons lounging on a group of big red rocks. A male much larger than the rest, and the strongest of them all, face upturned, looks up, and stares brashly back.

It is something! these rare occasions—and this is one of them—when a fresh breeze blows in off the Atlantic and fills the streets of New York City so that an afternoon in June becomes the epitome of something, and something in everyone arises to the occasion.

Isadora Duncan. Martha Graham. Merce Cunningham. Not unlike those troops of previous eras that become sets of toy soldiers, whole sets of troupes of modern dancers now flood the Christmas toy market. It is noted with amusement and amazement—but without comprehension—that boys, as well as girls, like to play with the troupes of dancers, and that they are toys that boys and girls play with together. But note that significance: like the first step in a performance of a complicated dance it may mark a first sign, an initial intimation, a revelation in miniature of the peaceable nature of man—a noteworthy minor beginning of peace without end among men of all nations.

He builds a flamboyant chandelier that sets aflame stars at the ends of its arms, builds beauty with bits of cobalt glass that can tinkle in a breeze, and sends solid black shadows of trembling shapes and bright purple forms dancing on white walls, where crystals coalesce into worms of light and rainbow-splash from candles swinging in porcelain cups of fragile freckleware.

The Pocatello Idaho Potato Parade is led each year, not by a Queen, but by the King of Potatoes, carried not by a coach, but by white horses drawing a perfectly plain, open wooden wagon, perfect for the display of a gigantic potato.

Hunger of the fishmonger for a good steak is his motivation for breaking the law, for being a thief, so that he could sit in a regular restaurant, first having something strong in a small glass, before eating red meat, that would be capped by a beautiful giant portobello mushroom.

The baseball game starts at 4:30 in the afternoon, two hours late. The game has been postponed on account of rain, but now it begins in earnest—each side scoring three or four runs in each inning, until at the end of nine innings the score is tied 24-24, and it continues tied until the 14th inning, when it begins to rain again, but now it begins in earnest.

There's nothing about it to do when they shout it. He stands on a barrel and yodels and carols, singing songs in a tavern on the night before Christmas. He'd be damned if he did it, and dunned if he didn't, so he empties the barrel by turning the spigot, and a tightfisted nitwit picks a fight with a slob. Merry Christmas!

On a gorgeous evening in Summer—we are lying on the grass at midnight behind the spotlights on the Main Library lawn that illuminate the marble face of the long building across the top of which is a lofty-sounding sentence in prose written in stone using two-foot-high capital letters, that contains a grammatical error.

Schools & Flocks is the title of the documentary demonstrating the similarity of movement en masse of fish and birds.

At a girls' boarding school a tall freshman socks her smaller sister—who is a sophomore—on her sister's birthday, gives her a black eye as a birthday present, and as a result is herself expelled for being an undesirable girl.

That strangest of shelves at the top of the closet is chock-full of boxes and packages wrapped in brown paper, that are never taken down, that have been sitting there for years from those strange days of long ago that are so hard to imagine and practically impossible to remember.

The great American escape artist and magician is a child prodigy and his earliest feat is the tying of a knot. The remarkable boy masters the tying of his shoelaces without removing his mittens.

She cuts apart the patches from a patchwork quilt, and makes potholders from the pieces, which at Christmastime she mails as presents to relatives.

After it has been set afire by lightning he buys the wholesale jewelry factory in New Jersey cheap, but though he's gotten a bargain, now he's got to string a thousand necklaces and sort ten thousand earrings into five thousand piles of pairs.

I go the wrong way, and at the stairs I go up instead of down, at a fork I go left instead of right, and then again take the wrong turn, and if I have to repeat it, I won't forget it, I'll do it the same way again.

Bushels of buttercups bundled in bales and loaded on an old wooden wagon are hauled by an elderly horse to the barge that is pulled by a strong donkey along the canal that wends its colorful wonderful way.

A poplar is crossed with a pine to get an evergreen with white bark that loses its needles each Spring, and regains them in the Autumn, growing quickly each Winter, it lies dormant during the Summer. Soon there is a forest of them, and in ten years it is determined that all animals in the forest of trees that have been crossed are cross-eyed, including the scientists, and the person writing this.

On the day the cat wanders off the dog also vanishes. That evening the young couple goes out searching for their pets, and are never seen again. Although I've rented their apartment, I'll not go looking for a dog or a cat.

The most extraordinary animals in South America are half a dozen species of the most ordinary small Atlantic Ocean fish that live in a saltwater swamp that is the source of the Amazon River on an Andean plateau several miles above sea level in the highlands of Central Peru.

The Leaping Vine slides slowly horizontally along long branches—then leaps to an adjacent tree, where it continues to travel parallel to the ground on its horizontal trip, traveling from tree to tree.

He buys an acre of land and builds an eight-foot wall around it. There is a door in the wall, much like the front door of a house. All along the inside of the wall, he plants many varieties of flowering vines. At the four corners of the wall he builds four rooms.

Sludge from the mineworks slides down a mountain, joined by boulders and rocks caught in its falling, and as the avalanche widens, picking up speed—trees are caught up in it and brought down with it, and at the bottom the branches are buried, the roots sticking up toward the sky.

The stranger who seeks the hermit is greeted by quietness of morning fog on the small lake—anything beyond fifty feet is invisible—while she seeks out his secret cottage which she knows to be the only building on the lake, a lonely building hidden among the willows that seem to wave welcome, and make the lonely only stranger.

There is a road in a woods on which grass grows between two ruts of sand and that is bordered by bushes and small trees that reach out to noisily touch cars that pass by. A mile down the road a stack of fifty unpainted telephone poles lies on the ground in a bunch. A huge truck has come and will deposit them along this road which runs through the woods on its way to a cluster of farms, along which they will be raised, one by one.

Hot air balloons, blimps and dirigibles fill the morning mountain sky in a celebration of Summer, while hang gliders softly careen among them in perfect picnic weather, all taking delight in updrafts—some landing on lakes on pontoons.

A diving bell sits on the bottom and bubbles, and its air hoses stretch to a ship at the surface. A sailor inside turns dials and adjusts parameters, while a scientist clicks cameras that are fastened to the hull, getting on film a milling parade of fish that pass by and of a ceiling of silhouettes between themselves and the sky, recording the swaying of plants on the floor, and schools that are darting, purple doggerel, colorful coral, and more.

The "icy darklings" are antarctic fireflies that live on the most southerly islands within the Antarctic Circle, hibernating among the roots of stunted trees bent over backwards during the long antarctic daytime, but becoming active during the windy darkness, whenever the winds of night don't blast and whirl or swirl too fast.

It could as well be gold. He is the foremost connoisseur and collector of fool's gold, as well as a recognized authority on that not uncommon, that very ordinary metal. His extensive exhibiting of his collection, fabulous geological specimens of consummate beauty, over the years brings him not only fame and fortune, but a happy marriage, as well, to the beautiful woman who is his assistant in the handling of his beloved stones.

The transformation of New York City begins with a banning of commercial vehicles on weekends, and soon on Sundays all motorized traffic ceases, and soon after that—with a penchant for the historical—a fad for horses becomes the fashion and an obssession of those who dub themselves the *new New Yorkers.* Soon skyscraper stables are accommodating a million horses, and horse-drawn carriages and brightly painted wagons happily jam the avenues and byways of the new New York.

The Lakes of Canada is the title, and it is comprised of as many large illustrated volumes as an encyclopedia and in them every lake in Canada is described, lovingly, meticulously, completely. The geology, history and general information are detailed. Not one lake is left out.

Its location near a desolate fjord along the coast of Norway was once known—but no longer. Called the Drain of Death, it was a salt-water whirlpool which mysteriously had appeared at the bottom of a well dug during the days of the Vikings, and in those times people to be punished by death were dropped into it.

For a flat fee I get a job painting a twenty-story fire escape orange—from top to bottom—and after finishing it, before getting paid, I discover I am expected to give it a second coat.

Three hundred and eighty-four dimes hidden in a cigar box in a basement behind a heat duct—it is the life savings of a dead ten-year-old boy, assiduously saved from what he had earned on his newspaper route twenty years ago, suddenly discovered after all these years by a repairman, who immediately turns the box over to the owners of the house, the boy's parents. The elderly man and woman spread out the dimes in piles of ten on the kitchen table, counting them out with a strange astonishment, and she says to her husband, "What a treasure!"

An albino cat without fur purrs in falsetto and is purchased for ten thousand dollars at the Dublin Cat Show by a millionaire for his young albino daughter.

There is neither jingle nor jangle to the mangle of a silver necklace that has been crushed by a ten-wheel ten-ton tractor-trailer truck after a box containing it has been tossed out onto a highway from a back seat of a silver convertible by an angry young woman.

Here are somewhat shaded ladies under dappled shadows of an oak that with a spacious spread of branches cloaks a meeting place. It is a Summer Club consuming lemonade and cups of tea, meeting here throughout the nineteenth century, where organdy is *de rigueur* and silks are out of place. The tree is as if waiting to be struck by lightning.

A hyperdermic needle is used to fill a ping-pong ball with mercury, and then it falls and gets lost down behind the cushions of the davenport.

He is able to earn a living selling a sawdust sandwich on a ramp at a dock that boats carrying tourists use when visiting Sandwich Island of the New Hebrides in the Southwest Pacific. He would take a photo of a tourist pretending to take a bite of the incredible, inedible sandwich, and the photo would be immediately printed on a postcard which bore the inscription, "Eating a sandwich on Sandwich Island!" Some tourists would buy a dozen postcards, and that single joke suffices to support his large family for his lifetime.

After occupants of a summer cottage turn off the lights and go to a movie in town, their goldfish spends an evening watching a firefly that hovers about the spherical fishbowl.

The ugly, digusting pipsqueak scampers about, scouring the rocks and devouring lichen and moss, quickly licking them up with a terrible tongue that rasps, a purple tongue that consists of several spotted yellow lobes with hundreds of tiny orange daggers embedded in beds of scarlet needles, and that makes a squeaking noise when scouring the surface of a rock. Its only fur grows out from inside its ears and at the tip of its tail.

A large blonde horse with a large black spot on its flank gallops down an empty street at dawn, as if headed for its stable, and disappears in the distance around a corner.

The praise for a chef who wins the prize is that he takes the cake, for this winner serves a can of Campbell's Cream of Tomato Soup and floats numerous slices of fresh tomato on its surface, each a different color.

It takes the ten-year-old no more than ten minutes to make a paper airplane, and then she sails it over the edge of the Grand

Canyon and for twenty minutes—with field glasses—she watches it descend and finally land on a rock among the rapids of the Colorado River.

There's nothing cuter than a baby cassowary—in the opinion of its mother, who is flightless, and the largest and toughest bird in Australia, and can flatten a mule with one kick, and who can inspire fear in a herd of giant fighter-kangaroos.

Although it's on the edge of my consciousness, although it's on the tip of my tongue, I know it's gone forever. Last night I awoke several times with the same dream—on a blazing desert I heard a lovely voice pronounce *the title* for this book, but now I can't remember it and I know I never will. On a blazing desert I've been deserted by that voice, and must now be satisfied with the desert's brilliant silence.

A puma, a panther, a cougar, a catamount and a mountain lion meet on a Montana mountainside, each arousing in the others a friendly curiosity. That evening they hunt together, and during the following day the five of them sleep in a heap in a cave, like kittens curled up in a ball.

A rocking chair flies through the air, thrown by an angry woman off a porch of a houseboat into the center of a stream that sends it out to sea, a bobbing perch for a happy pelican.

She is a professional nanny for children of guests at The Posh Hotel. She holds a swizzle stick between her fingers and draws large letters in the air for the children to guess the words she might be writing. They are rewarded with jelly beans.

The logjam allows lions to cross an African stream, which races and rages beneath tumbled trunks of tropical hardwood trees worth a fortune downstream in the city.

There is an undercover old folks home (location utterly unknown) for *spies,* for elderly men and women who have been intimately involved in secret operations by our government, for it is deemed prudent to keep an eye on them—many are dangerous customers—and to keep careful tabs on the old codgers.

It is a terrific tale within a fantastic story that a Toronto storyteller relates, standing by a fireplace of a huge log cabin where a roaring fire illuminates his audience of twenty boys and girls.

Thunder and lightning punctuate his sentences. One by one they fall asleep.

A submarine enters New York Harbor on Independence Day with flags flying, leading a parade of tall sailing ships, with a drum and bugle corps performing on its narrow deck, and the musicians continue their performance with great concentration, although the submarine is unexpectedly swept by a strong current, and as if at the center of a whirlpool it spins in a circle three times, and is rammed by the largest sailing ship.

It is an island where animals are allowed to grow old, where there are no carnivores. The island is populated entirely by animals which will die of the diseases of old age.

The frame is worth more than the painting, for an old wooden frame on a poorly executed five-century-old painting has been carved as a favor to his patron Lorenzo de' Medici by Michaelangelo.

The Fraternity of Fools at the best of schools is at first an informal association of students with poor marks who find friendship and feel more comfortable with those like themselves, and it is only later that they learn that their liking for their peers is a perilous preoccupation.

Above a Norwegian fjord on a cliff a sunbeam sits upon a sparkling stone.

Two gigantic jewels: An uncut pyramidal emerald, unclouded and the size of a small green parrot, is perched and perfectly balanced atop a perfect pearl the size of an ostrich egg, set on the surface of a large bowl of sand. Perhaps because the final bid sets a record at that London auction house—when the auctioneer cries, "Sold!"—his gavel is brought down with unpremeditated violence and the emerald falls off the pearl, falls harmlessly into the sand, while onlookers gasp and the audience en masse falls into a fit of infectious giggling.

The Good Line
& 63 untitled paragraphs

What if I were to be thrown a good line?—What would I do with it? Let it lie on a piece of paper in the center of the table? Or would I make copies of it, and send it to various people? Or I could carry copies with me in my shirt pocket, and when I'd meet various people, I would say, "Would you like to see a good line?" and take a copy from my shirt pocket, and I would add, "Here!" as I handed over the sheet of paper on which the good line is written.

After her awful operation, she balances her gallstone on her birthstone and keeps them under a bell jar on her desk at work.

A robin takes a bath in a rainbow in the mist of a circling sprinkler on the lawn.

The rabid raccoon ate a tainted potato and died of food poisoning while frothing at the mouth in the jaws of a trap.

An agent for fashion models installs funhouse mirrors in his waiting room.

The Tunnel of Love bursts into flames in a carnival catastrophe inadvertently caused by a discarded cigar of the Bearded Lady.

Fat folk dance with an elegance of elephants with twisting trunks.

In a *Cartoon Noire* a black automobile runs over a black squirrel in the dead of night.

When a four-flusher meets a finagler they each immediately recognize that they look alike—it is love at first sight.

A folded-up newspaper is flung up onto a front porch by a boy on a luminous bike that passes by in the dark.

To make wine in a washtub, he crushes a bushel of luscious squashes with his feet in galoshes.

He does his doctorate on charismatic people, on famous actors and on infamous dictators.

At 3:15 a.m. the luminous dial on my old-fashioned wristwatch is all I can see of myself in the full-length mirror.

When the dead want to play, they go to Argentina and become proficient with the bola.

For her birthday he gives her an antique silver Spanish thimble as a vase for a bouquet of four-leaf clovers.

He dips a dozen different gorgeous blossoms in batter and deep fries them in a wok.

The dominion of delight is adjacent to the dolorous domain of perpetual pain.

Is there a closer grocer?

A laser light at midnight plays upon a Broadway beauty's Easter bonnet.

I have an extensive collection of cornerstones purchased for small sums from the wreckers of big buildings.

A doorstop in the form of a foot-high iron frog has been sitting on the doorstep of a French castle on the River Nône for six centuries.

Sawdust freshly strewn covers a filthy floor between the spitoons in preparation for the morning sweep by a burly bartender.

The green cardinal fills a backyard with her beautiful song.

He dreams he's dancing and that he is singing to his partner, until his wife wakes him up, complaining of his snoring.

I am a collector of images and deal in ideas—a hatful of my trinkets are spread out on a blanket and offered to all to consider.

The bigamist dreams of four mothers-in-law.

Petrified pillows of lava appear on an ocean floor a hundred yards off the coast of Iceland, disturbing the sleep of nearby townsfolk.

It is unwise to question the sagacity of wise men.

The chiropractor pounds vigorously on the back door.

He cut up a flagpole for kindling, and when winter came he discovered that it wouldn't burn.

It is enough to make a man smile, the facial expression on a gorilla contemplating the grin of a crocodile.

He lives in a world of silhouettes in which nothing casts a shadow.

Hundreds of inhabited planets encircle a single star, so that the sky from any one of them seems full of many moons of different sizes.

The nimble stumble among orange patterns of the autumn puddle.

A girl plunges her arm into a bushel of navy beans.

A mop stands in a bucket and leans against a wall, meditating, contemplating the floor.

The Tottenville potatoes grow without visible eyes.

In Ireland on the Dingle Peninsula the gravel path along the cliff must not be walked on in the rain.

A gigantic silver fish with transparent eyes appears beneath a glass-bottom boat.

The not-so-distant drums beat wildly on my neighbor's stereo.

A startling red cliff appears out of the blue from the midst of the mist on the green Arkansas River.

Protected somewhat from crashing surf, six rowdies in a rowboat ride out a drenching rainstorm underneath a battered wooden wharf.

In conducting a lie detector test, an investigator who takes truth serum will ask the right questions.

The opera singer clutches her throat when the baritone sings a sour note.

A Carolina cow with a sore throat makes a moo this morning more like a moaning.

An Hungarian player is the chess champion of Chile where he lives like a king and swims in the cold Pacific among swarms of anchovies.

She crochets brown doilies that look exactly like pancakes and waffles.

Flat from Texas, spherical from Spain, little ones from Long Island—it is of onions which we speak, which make us weep.

She walks through crashing surf holding a seashell to her ear.

All her cat books are dog-eared.

She knits a sweater for her grandson's baby alligator out of yarn sold especially for knitting bathing suits.

The gait of the walker along the Tomahawk Trail turns into something like a solo fox-trot.

The giant basketball player chews five pieces of gum at the same time while shooting baskets one after the other.

He's a slugger in the slammer, a mugger in the manner of a late-at-niqht jumper, and he belongs in jail.

The only things broken during an earthquake are the delicate legs of a table whose top is a slab of stone.

I have a complete list of all animals that sing and half-hour tapes of each song.

It is a noisy pantomime.

There are those certain things that can only be seen out of the corner of the eye.

A seagull lands on the head of a walrus, who doesn't notice.

The fingers of both my hands hug a slender glass of claret, while a tomato from my garden sits sliced upon a plate of scarlet glass.

A frying pan drops on the floor and two eggs slide over-light onto the carpet.

He rounds a corner and crosses a circle and then circles a square, but then bashes his bumper on a fire hydrant.

I got kicked by a cassowary, and I've never been the same...that's why I write like this, always different. It's the cassowary kick.

A boulder is transported a great distance on an Ice Age glacier which on melting drops the erratic traveler in what is to become a Massachusetts meadow, places it precisely atop a smaller taller rock, where it remains balanced for ten thousand years. During that time the surface of the bottom rock becomes completely covered with a thick mat of dark green moss, while brilliantly colored yellow, orange, purple and red lichen grow all over the larger stone.

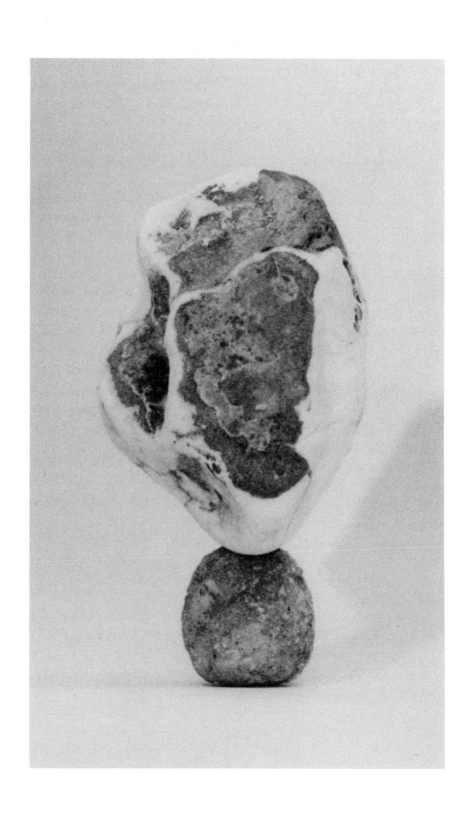

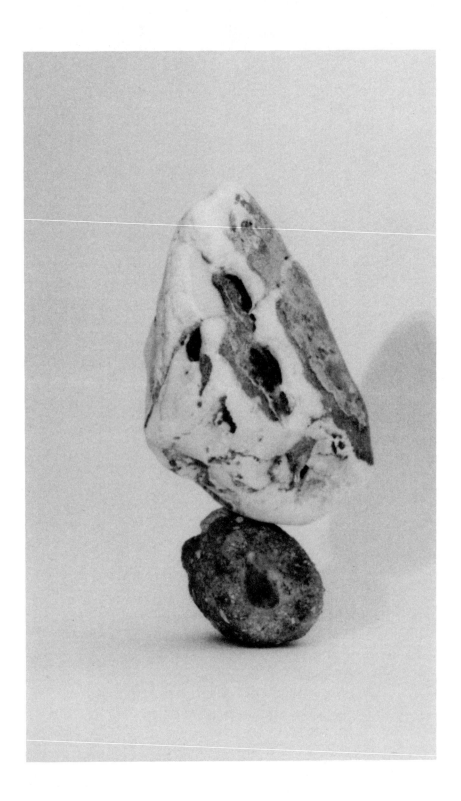

PART SIX: 64 PARAGRAPHS

Floating Notes of the Sooty Wastrels
& 63 untitled paragraphs

There is a syncopation of frogs and a noisiness of crickets in the Garden of the Goldfish Pond where pairs of balanced boulders, partially submerged, put their heads above water as if in calm appreciation of the flutey floating notes from the throats of Sooty Wastrels, which nest among the thistles in the thicket of thorns.

Fearless fashion models riding thoroughbreds pell-mell down a dry riverbed though a ghost town are being followed and photographed by terrified camera crews in helicopters, who are all afraid of flying.

About to rain buckets at any moment, the summer evening air is electric...a lightning bug lands on a lightning rod at the same time lightning strikes it.

Tugboats twinkle in the twilight and harbor bouys ding-dong, as a ghostly black ocean liner slips between them silent, solemn, Carribean-bound, full of drunken tourists, already many dancing.

The phone is at an open window, and she is speaking on it. A sweetly singing bird lands upon the telephone line which stretches from a telephone pole out at the highway to a small pole attached to the side of the house, above the window where she sits. It is a small finch with a splendid song, with a red mark on its face. On the phone, she says "I'm sorry. What were we talking about?"

A Raggedy Ann doll on the back seat of a four-door sedan in the darkest shadows of the gray garage awaits the return of the little girl who had been carried into the house the night before, asleep on the shoulder of her father.

In the Great Northern Wilderness where grizzly bears abound, where a wolfpack revels in its howls and giant cougars come for dinner, the Conservation Officer sleeps in a cage.

Floods & Droughts is the title of the book, *A History of the Five Greatest of Each,* a large picture book for a low coffee table.

When the royal cat has a gorgeous kitten the Queen says it must be named Prince Charming, but the Princess calls it Crazy Horse.

At the front of a huge Justice Department Building a brisk breeze blows a front page of a newspaper, sends it swirling at the height of second-story windows, so that it wraps itself around the head and shoulders of a stone lady on a pedestal, who already has a blindfold.

She saws off a limb which holds a hornet's nest that overhangs a stream. The nest and branch drop into the water, and slowly float away in a manner lacking the rapidity, but making more noise than a speedboat.

A baby burro, belonging to a next-door neighbor in a small town in Southern Mexico, adopts a childless American couple. The pair has come to Mexico to adopt a child, but because they do not have a regular income, being artists, the Mexican adoption agency refuses them. They purchase the friendly burro, and their pet becomes the center of their lives, and figures prominently in their paintings for a number of years.

The young son of a shoestore clerk uses a shoehorn as a scoop and fills a shoebox with sand to take home from the beach to keep in his bedroom. He ties the cover of the box on tight with a leather shoelace from a knee-high woodsman's boot.

A geyser appears in a Wyoming schoolyard from a hole where they are trying to put in place a twenty-five-foot flagpole. But before they can insert the pole the geyser shoots a steady steaming fountain seventy-five feet into the air for three minutes, before it pauses for five. Then the three-minute fountain reappears, and quickly the steamy cycle becomes established, and eventually the smalltown schoolyard becomes a national park.

Walking in the dark with high heels clicking on the tiles adjacent to the swimming pool, the movie star from the early '40s, herself now in her eighties, is once more transmogrified into a leopard—an ancient arthritic, limping leopard—as the clicking of her heels becomes suddenly silent, and the darkness of time closes in.

He puts together expensive survival kits for fortune hunters headed out into expanses of wilderness.

A big sticky bubble of a toasted jellyfish collapses into a South Pacific pancake, which is great with maple syrup.

The trapeze turns into smoke and he falls to the net.

There are several kinds of flowers in several sorts of vases in a room that has giant flowers on the wallpaper. There are purple anomalies, red rainspouts, blue butterspoons, as well as orange iffies, columbones and small bespeckled violet jugworts. At the center of the round room on a round table fruit flies hover above a circular platter of plums.

Poison ivy luxuriantly covers bare limbs of a giant dead oak completely.

Injured by angels, a girl with four breasts who sings at a circus wears a double-breasted suit, a gold fedora and twirls a gray pin-striped candy cane with one hand, while holding a microphone with the other.

This chest of old toys, all perfectly painted like new, was found in an attic by my grandfather when he was a boy and had belonged to his father's youngest brother, who had died as a child. The toys had been treasured and cherished by the boy's father (my grandfather's grandfather) who had on some sad and rainy afternoons taken them out to play with, solemnly and fondly, and they have always been kept in this pristine condition.

They were jumping out of trees, leaping over streams and climbing on cliffs, but playing hopscotch with the girls was my only game. Now those girls are grown women who themselves are jumping out of trees and leaping over streams and climbing on cliffs, so the hopscotch of the mind is the only game, and I play it all the same.

Where streets are narrow and buildings tall, the sky is skinny.

As eyes open they glimpse for a moment a panoramic view of many miles of the Greenland Glacier, but after a long and thoughtful blink, the eyes open again to the white expanse—this time determined to be a piece of typing paper, on the edge of which my head reclines, the both of us, paper and I, are lying on my bedroom rug.

The dancers rise in ghostly garb, smoke writhes upon the stage in colored lights and the note of a flute is afloat from the back of the standing-room-only audience....

In what is a largely unpopulated place in the western part of Central Peru near a trickling brook that soon becomes the Marañón River (that is, the source of the Amazon), at the foot of a small extinct volcano, the searcher finally finds his fortune at the foot of a tree in the form of a solid gold left foot, life size. And now thousands of searchers are swarming over the once pristine land, each searching for the right foot.

The excellent sculptor becomes a serial killer. As a child he covered balsa wood frames of his model airplanes with wings of monarch butterflies.

An old man who waxes a dance floor is alone in the huge room, and when he finishes, removes his workshoes, revealing red socks—and wearing the red socks, performs a peculiar dance for five minutes.

Fondly did the fine old lady look upon the laughing little boy rising on wave after wave, a parent holding a hand on either side, everybody looking and laughing at grandmother on the beach dressed in black.

He makes a mint from his invention of a machine that manufactures millions of bubbles in a variety of geometric shapes from doughnuts to crystals. Foam consisting entirely of bubbles shaped like doughnuts feels quite different against the skin than foam made from pyramid-shaped bubbles, or foam in the form of spaghetti.

A nine-year-old boy in Trinidad slides down a grassy slope on a cardboard box, and as he starts to trudge upward for another slide is astonished by an earthquake which begins an avalanche on the hillside—not of falling rocks—of a steady rain of pebbles, so that soon from below a plume of red chalk dust arises, the chalky stuff covering him as if he's been dipped into a scarlet dye. His mother is astonished at the sight of him, and bursts into tears on seeing him safe.

A doctor declares him a suicide. He was not a success, but his scariest failure is his hair-raising treatment for baldness, which kills him.

Oranges drop of their own accord from the Florida trees at the proper season for the small field has been abandoned by its owner, who has become an invalid and gone North to live near his children on the Upper Peninsula of Michigan.

That loveliest of women takes delight in peach jam made by her aunt in Japan every August, and mailed to America without fail by her cousin, whom she had played with as a child in the orchard.

The fragrance of afternoon wafts by on a Summer breeze from the lake, and has already a taste of Fall...are we ready to go home?

Who. The noisy dancers have webbed feet and adhesive suckers on their toes. It is the annual anuran display of cold-blooded romance—as tree frogs dance upon a branch above the pool, the big-eyed owl swoops down. Who. Who.

In the Bay of Fundy where tides are high and can quickly rise forty feet, big fish can be caught in big puddles which can quickly come into existence as a falling tide reaches Low. Old Penobscot Indians and young Canadian boys stand beside each other, and fish with spears.

On the Upper Peninsula of Michigan ten duck hunters are shot dead at dawn by a deranged member of the Audubon Society who escapes to a desolate Far Northern Canadian lake where ducks that wind up migrating each Spring end up spending the Summer. Though he is never apprehended, neither can he return to civilization. He is unable to migrate south with the ducks in the Fall, and freezes to death in a blizzard on the lake during the Winter.

At noon all over town certain chemicals sprinkled onto burning logs cause chimneys to emit thick plumes of either bright green or brilliant orange smoke for an hour on St. Patrick's Day.

The charm of the snake charmer is working on *me*. I am tapping my foot as he plays a tin whistle, and in a moment I shall begin to dance. He is playing my scales, and I lick—at the same time—each of his eyes with my forked tongue. When the small boy climbs up the rope and vanishes, I know where he is.

He makes a mint making men's bell-bottom trousers with French cuffs so that cuff links sporting large moonstones might be worn at the ankles, to match much smaller moonstones adorning cuff links at the wrists.

A very ancient cutting stone (covered with red ochre) which long ago had been used to dig out the wood of a dugout canoe is found by a rather ancient archeolgist who determines its age by carefully studying sediments above and below the location where she has found it.The woman is an expert in her field, and she wears lots of red ochre rouge and lipstick. Though her three graduate students study her carefully, it is not possible to determine her age.

Leaving the brilliant morning sunshine behind, she dreams three workmen enter a giant open pipe (12 feet in diameter) under construction, that when completed will carry water from the mountains to the city. A long line of water three inches deep at the bottom of the pipe stretches back a hundred yards through the darkness. There is no stranger danger in the world than the world inside the pipe, where a water moccasin waits, a grizzly bear has come to give birth to twin cubs and sleeping rabid bats hang in a long line along the top of the tube, and without thinking, one of the workmen grabs a bunch of deadly daffodils that have a foul odor caused by their growing in a bed of poisoned putrid soil.

Though they both like to climb and carry pretty much the same equipment, they have nothing else in common, and never do both. He who takes delight in climbing down through deep caves and his brother the mountain climber are the opposite of twins.

The palms of the piccolo player's hands become incurably covered with thumb-bunions, pimply scabs, warts and chronically infected corns, and so he becomes a music critic, dictating his reviews to his wife, who is tone deaf.

The zookeeper's wife likes to cook and makes treats for the animals. Depending on the nature of their ordinary diets, she invents different desserts and snacks for each type of animal. The elephants had once belonged to a circus, and at the sight of her they perform a series of circus tricks. At her appearance the bears stand up and walk all around the cage on their hind legs, not taking their eyes off her, seeming to be smiling. When the parrots see her they begin speaking Chinese, repeating phrases learned in their native land. When she stands at the edge of the cage of the tigers, their purring can be heard all over the zoo.

Day begins in a downright way, fog lifts off the lake at dawn, and the woods fill up with the noise of birds, and the odor of coffee wafts over from a campfire near the canoe, which has been pulled out of the water a little. A dog comes out of the tent to sit by the fire, and the whole world begins to dance, the leaves begin to dance upon the boughs, the trees to sway, and from inside the tent a violin begins to play a partita by Bach.

At a time during the last decade of the nineteenth century at a dinner at the Chinese embassy the ambassador provides his English and American guests with ivory and gold chopsticks that have at their tips—carefully carved—tiny left and right hands with outstretched fingers.

A cranky curmudgeon falls in love with a crochety dwarf, a fussy seamstress who crochets, who makes a mint designing and sewing clothes for small people and those whose figures are deformed. They are a perfect pair.

Lying for hundreds of years in the dark in a dry and inaccessible cave high on a face of a cliff overlooking the Indian Ocean their colors as brilliant as ever—forty huge flags of European kingdoms, neatly folded by pirates in the seventeenth century and since then untouched and unseen, now rest in a rusty chest, undiscovered.

His best-selling bicycle horn emits the call of a whooping crane, and the horn that he sells for a motorcycle makes the sound of a trumpeting elephant, but the tiniest electrical gadget of all is a horn for small cars which in the middle of a traffic jam can make a most marvelous moan—that deepest of sonorous groans— the sound of a foghorn on an ocean liner.

The mysterious man has a tattoo on his wrist in an accurate shape of a wristwatch, and each numeral is clearly discernable on the purple mirror image of the clockface.

It is a statistical fluke—practically nobody dies for a year in a small town and so the cemetery goes bankrupt, and the only death in town is the suicide of the owner of the funeral parlor.

It is held in such secrecy that neither you nor I have ever heard of it—an annual costume contest at the clandestine *Detectives'*

Dance in New York City on Halloween. Every year they dress the same: wives are obliged to attend dressed up as motorcycle patrolmen and must wear boots, handcuffs and sunglasses, while the detectives, themselves, every year come dressed as adagio dancers, and each must wear a striped shirt and beret. Winners and their spouses on the following February get a three-day expenses-paid trip to New Orleans to attend the Mardi Gras. Of course, this is not true. There are many female detectives, and it might be wondered what costume they wear. I don't know. Perhaps they go to work that night.

She has a hippopotamus tattooed upon each hip, just behind and below the bone at the outermost tips of her pelvis. He has two giraffes that face each other tattooed upon his upper chest, leaning against his collarbone, their necks go up on either side of his throat so that their heads hide behind his ears, and are tattooed on the backs of his ears, so that their noses touch the backs of his earlobes.

A landscape designer dies and what later is attributed to his genius should in fact be ascribed to his poor penmanship and an inability of workmen to read his plans, for in redesigning the park at the center of town they plow the paths and plant flowers where the paths should be, leaving many islands of lawn, at the last minute made accessible by numerous low wooden bridges.

In The Village he awoke at five every day before dawn, at the same time rain or shine, without using an alarm clock. Each morning with his tea he'd take a few little chunks of Cheddar, each matched by tiny chunks of tinned fruit, with an English muffin. During most of a lifetime in London he'd been a late riser, without using an alarm clock, awakening each morning at ten, Greenwich Time—that is, at 5 a.m., Greenwich Village time.

Piercing the Western wilderness on the gold-rush trail, one rainy morning many mules refuse to move. They dig in their heels, and whinny. They shake off their heavy loads, stand on their hind legs, with whinnies like screams. One by one they run, rush out onto open land, down muddy canyons, and upward over hilly terrain, racing in drenching rain, terrified by lightning and thunder, never to be seen again.

There is glare off the glaze on the gravel on the Road of the Morning Moon, and on fog in the fields floating out from a lake and filling the forest, spilling out onto an empty highway where it crosses a deserted dirt road, all damp with dew before dawn. A hitchhiker walks steadily along, bathed by cold brilliant moonlight of a starry cloudless sky portending more dazzling discomfort of another hot Summer day.

He has a date for dinner and he will concentrate on not eating too much. The eye of the bathroom scale winks in the afternoon when the shadow of the fat man falls across it as he leans forward toward the mirror above the sink to shave—he has a heavy five-o'clock shadow,

There is a sophisticated, complicated and kaleidoscopic continuous light show in a restaurant mostly patronized by the deaf, where waitresses are proficient at sign language, as is the cook and are busboys.

Riding on a subway to the end of the line, I then walk upstairs to the street and catch a bus which I ride as far as it will take me. I am the last passenger on the bus, when the driver says, "End of the line!" I don't know where I'm going, but I know what I'm going to do. I locate a highway heading out of town, and I try to hitch a ride, but without success—so I begin to walk. I have money in my pocket, and I don't need anything else. It's a warm and sunny Spring morning, and I'm on my way.

The cemetery for lifelong couples is a grove of balanced boulders, each double grave adorned by a pair of tombstones—of large inscribed boulders, one balanced on the other.

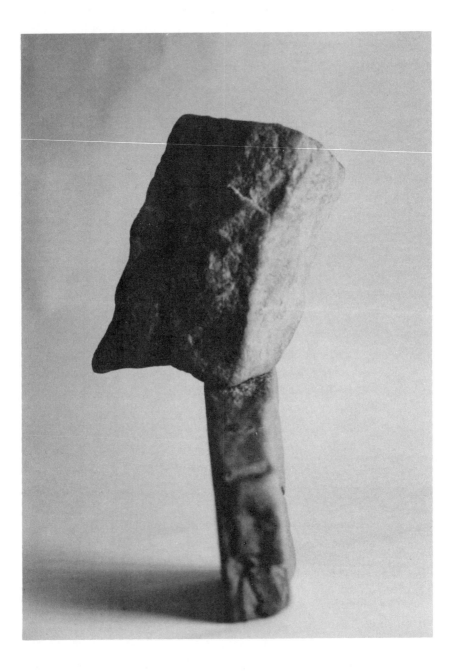

Pleasures of the Imagination
64 Beginnings

For Sally Gross

There are different kinds of writing. For instance, there's the kind of writing where you walk over to the typewriter, sit down, and write a first line. You go into the kitchen for a glass of water, light a cigarette, all the while thinking of what you've written. You return to the typewriter and write a second line, then you write a third line, and oh—all sorts of things happen, and there—you find you've written the last line, and if what you've written is any good, then it's all of a piece, as if the whole thing were implicit in the beginning.

As if you put your hand in the water and catch a fish by the tail.

However, there is a different kind of writing: you sit down at the typewriter, just as before, and write a beginning. But when it comes to writing more—nothing happens. You have many thoughts, your mind is aswim with phrases, but your hands don't move toward the keys. Finally, you begin again, and write a new first line.

I have a big old wire wastebasket which I never empty in which I put things that I think I might work more on, and over a number of years it's got chock full of beginnings, false starts, some might say—failures perhaps—but I've made a book of them, or what-you-might-call a book, of sixty-four examples of this nameless genre of writing. And I have given them names, just as if they were regular stories.

Sometimes I wonder whether there are real stories implicit in such first lines—you might say virtual stories, not unreal, but existing in some never-never realm not inaccessible perhaps to certain readers who do themselves indulge in the pleasures of the imagination.

In London

In London yesterday a lorry lunged, sideswiped a fog light and plunged into the Thames. The plainclothesman who surreptitiously was following me broke cover, took a whistle from beneath his cloak and blasted the alarm, rushing to the embankment, abandoning me in the yellow fog.

The Miserable Ostrich

Walking down a desert road in a sandstorm, a six-foot ostrich with a painful broken toe staggered with the wind behind him, wagged his wings wildly each time his left foot touched the sand, until finally, for the first time in his life—indeed, for the first time in ten million years—the ostrich flew like an ordinary bird, rose two hundred feet into the air, soared for five minutes here and there....

Croak!

The red berries of Fall—each scarlet ball rebounds the colors of the call of the scarlet tanager. Green frog—CROAK!—the water lily on which he sits trembles, and a careful eye could see green rings radiate around it, startling a dozing dragonfly.

An iridescent insect walks by.

Gong

It's hard to hold a hammer with your arm in a sling while carrying a gong during the rush hour on the subway in Tokyo.

The Floodwaters

The floodwaters left a ring on the outside of the bathtub.

The Daymoon

A racing fog enveloped the ship for a number of minutes, a stinging mysterious mixture of mist and hail making haloes of rainbows around the golden white lights of the ship.

It is the boat of my dream! But this cold railing is no dream....

Last night, while sleeping I dreamed that I looked across a bay, or perhaps it was a wide river, and I saw a large yacht, a streamlined boat with perhaps eight portholes along its side, and in my hands I held a miniature replica of the same boat. It was about a foot long. Somebody said, "It's the *Daymoon.*"

The Opera Singer's Vacation

On her vacations the famous opera singer lived alone in a cottage on a small island where she practiced to her heart's delight, and she could be heard at all hours like a faraway bird by wild animals on the most distant shores of the Canadian lake, which lay at the bottom of an uninhabited valley. The silence at the center of a becalmed lake is for her the most beautiful sound in the world.

The Arsonist at the Zoo

The poisonous orange salamander of Peru in its glass cage at the Staten Island Zoo attracted the gaze of the arsonist (wearing blue sneakers and carrying a rope in his belt), who had broken in at midnight to start a fire, but had become distracted from his insane design by the liveliness of the nocturnal animals; not that they were wild or especially noisy—they were merely awake and alert. The great cats were playing with their cubs, the raccoons were chasing each other, the primates played quiet games, and the place was alive with moving reptiles. After an hour he left without having started a fire, and he never returned to that scene of what could have been his worst crime.

And he never set another fire, but he became a drunk, closing the bars each night and staggering home at dawn.

There is something about us, we who are nocturnal, that nobody can ever understand.

A Lady of London

That seer upstairs at her seances who got those ghosts going with their shrieks and moans and grisly sighs until it was hard for a body to think, and at all times of the night, and such early morning hours she kept with her blasted meetings, the little old lady of London! Thank god she's gone.

Coat of Arms

Once upon a time there was a coat of arms...an extraordinary garment constructed by a tailor-lady out of old coats customers had left at her shop and never called for—the coat had twelve arms altogether, gathered in a circle at the top, so that when worn, five limp sleeves hung down in front like elephant trunks, and five hung down in back like a crazy cape.

The coat had no opening in front, it was slipped on like a sweater, and indeed it had no front, for the wearer could turn it whichever way he pleased, this time choosing the velvet sleeves, or the next time perhaps thrusting his arms into the tweed, or the black plaid.

The Flabbergasted Reader

The flabbergasted reader closed the book but held it in his hands, turning the book this way and that, studying the edges of the pages almost as if he were reading the title on the binding, all the while musing, pursing his lips, shifting his weight from one foot to the other, full of thoughts, he touched his forehead, and outside the summer-evening silence began to shimmer with the sweetly insistent sound of giant raindrops.

The Tornado of Snow

The brilliant white funnel of the tornado of snow dances atop an iceberg, vividly undulating against a sky that is black and yellow and brown, while below in the bay a blue whale suddenly surfaces beneath a giant waterspout. The boat is bobbing so, I can hardly write....I think it's my turn to row.

The Orchid Grower

The orchid grower looked like his plants. Strange purples and browns blotched his complexion on livid wattles, flesh suspended like ear lobes from his forehead and cheeks, sprinkled with light white moles. He lived in his greenhouse, a rather large complex of buildings, a veritable labyrinth of glass roofs and walls where for years he had conducted a successful business in tulips and dahlias—but his pride was his orchids.

The Celestial Sirens

Riding, being carried, lifted by a high wind a thousand feet in the an, 10,000 katydids silently swarm on the wings of a great ascending glider, and suddenly, as the silent ship enters the white heart of a cumulus cloud, 10,000 katvdids, as one, burst into their joyous song resounding as sirens here where shadows swim in fog.

Cape Cod

Atop a sand dune at Cape Cod a girl in a red and brown dress waves a yellow scarf. A crow and a seagull for a moment hover over her. Thunderclouds boil above them—they part, the seagull and the crow, and the clouds, and the sands are flooded with sunlight. At the foot of the dune stands a young Indian chief, and he raises his longbow in a graceful greeting. Taking great jumps, she rushes down the dune into his arms. At that very moment, on that very August afternoon, Lao-tse was born, but there it was midnight, and there was a New Moon.

Dishes

The obese puppeteer washed the dishes in the dark.

The Sacred Cow

The sacred cow stumbled in the mud, blinded by tropical rain, lurched forward onto the ooze, twisting its neck awry as it fell; and one of its long curved horns slipped between the roots of a tree, like a key in a lock, so that when it lumbered to its feet its horn was held fast and its snout pressed down into the mud; for five minutes it struggled and the next morning was found, a great white beast drowned in a puddle.

The Sunken Subway

On Thanksgiving Day the subway sank and the holiday riders stood in water up to their chests and then—single file—they all managed to escape up a ladder through a manhole that let them out at Herald Square into the midst of the Holiday Parade.

The Fans of van Gogh

I saw all the fans of van Gogh, all past and future ones, all the millions fluttering about in the air, making the sky black in back of him, all trying to get a peek over his shoulder as he sits there, very hungry, and looking not unlike a scarecrow in the sunshine in the middle of a wheat field, painting the crows.

I Thought You Were Writing

"I was afraid to say anything to you because I thought you were writing." It was his muse who spoke.

What Happens Next?

None of us could get out of the way.

There was nothing we could do.

Those ten seconds when we saw it coming toward us seemed an endless time.

There was no transition, no pain. Suddenly we were no longer there. We were here...listening to your story. But I don't mean to interrupt...you were telling us a story...what happens next?

The Ghost Town

About two hundred houses roasted in wreck under a Western sun.

Only wild cactus grew in the gardens.

The fence boards fell off and lay in their places, the gables were gray, and whole houses were weathering away. Not a speck of paint was visible.

Dust reigned.

Things with thorns flew through the hot air, and balls of tumbleweed raced through the empty streets.

Cucumbers

Cucumbers by the billion bombarded Paris, dropped from the skies by angry French peasants; they had hired a horde of Piper Cubs to fight a price war with their government; the cucumbers fell down chimneys, fell into children's sand piles, landed on lovers in the park, hit thieves while at their second-story work, covered the lawn of the British embassy, pummeled tennis players, dropped into the poorhouse....

A Very Ancient Dwarf

He parted his beard in the middle, and tied the ends to his two big toes, but this only a very ancient dwarf can do.

An Imaginary Biography

"I should like to write a short biography of Poe pointing out that the heartbreaking miseries of his life were a hoax perpetrated by his publishers, and that he actually led a happily proper life, wintering in Samoa, playing in amateur theatricals in Paris, with a cook from Peking to placate his Epicurean appetite, he was a collector of objects made of mother-of-pearl, and danced too much, his wife said, with her maids when he returned home from his famous binges with young Baudelaire."

The Listening Reader

The old-fashioned key was as big as a pistol and weighed three-and-a-half pounds.

His bedroom was circular and it had no door.

The man had a dagger tattooed on his nose, and he slipped into bed without any clothes, donning earphones and spectacles, he adjusted his ashtray, got his book in hand and twirled the dial to "distress" on his short-wave radio, while beginning to read.

It is the lighthouse keeper of St. Lisle.

The Stamp Collectors

The brown stamp on the envelope was carefully removed by a jet of steam from a teakettle by the eight-year-old collector in Venezuela who had just received the letter from Pennsylvania, from an older collector who lived in a tiny house in the woods, who had been snowbound for three weeks, who had been a sailor since his youth and had become familiar with the oceans, for forty years the lookout in the crows'-nest of a clipper ship, come home old to his birthplace to die in comfort, whiling away the time, doting on his stamp book, cared for by two orphan girls; and with a fine Spencerian hand he kept up a constant correspondence with those living in many foreign lands—for he had a wife in Borneo, Alaska, Australia, Norway, India, Malta, and in China, as well as Venezuela.

All his grandchildren collected stamps.

What About *That?*

What about that? A broken arm, a black eye, amnesia...found raving drunk in a cheap dive with your pockets full of diamonds.

Attic Animals

Walking up the narrow stairs, dark and dirty, to the brightly illuminated attic, afternoon sun ablaze through three windows, I saw a mole running in circles in a square of sunshine on the attic floor.

I had a feeling there was someone else in the room. I whirled around, and there sitting in a chair which had been covered with a sheet sat Beelzebub, my friend's cat, staring at the mole.

The attic was filled with the sound of buzzing flies.

Four Snow Leopards

Four snow leopards in transit by train to the Cincinnati zoo were by accident loosed from their cage, and unbeknownst to their sleeping keeper, they leaped from the slowly moving box-car at sunset, together disappearing into a Kansas field burgeoning with wheat that stretched as far as the eye could see. It was not until midnight, when the train pulled into the Chicago station, that their absence was discovered.

A small forest rose like an island in the sea of wheat. The leopards made for the trees. In a month there will he snow.

My Dentist Story

> "The book that glitters with mischief
> The writing most sparkling with glee
> The pages that jump at my touch—
> Your teeth—that is the book for me!"

...sang the mad dentist, dancing a jig on a tilted dental chair, shooting Novocain into the air; he made a leap for the ether and smashed it...to which all the dentists and nurses and attendants at the Northern Dispensary Clinic who had rushed to the scene, succumbed. He stood on the dental chair and stared in wonder and triumph at the dozen unconscious forms around him. As his co-workers slept their deep sleep, before he left them forever, to vanish into the labyrinth of the non-dental world, there to become a respectable old sculptor—he pulled all their teeth.

The Saloon

Where doppelgangers meet...that's the kind of saloon it was;

A Jumpy One

The evening was a jumpy one, the mosquitoes were insufferable, the distant drums were wild, their pet monkey spit in the soup, and so it was no wonder, what with the piano out-of-tune, their servant in tears, her best dress torn by a thorn, that the wife of the escaped convict was fed up.

The Fish and the Hermit

The verandah overlooked a canyon, the canyon held a thrashing stream, and in the stream there was a luminous fish, visible from above on dark nights, for which in his loneliness the hermit fished with a net on the end of a long, strong string.

The only shining object in the dilapidated shack was a large empty fish tank filled with water and illuminated by a deep-purple bulb. Indeed, it was the way the fish imagined heaven, much spookier and quieter than nature.

How they yearned for each other, these two, on such different levels.

The fish tried to imagine how the devil he could climb the string.

The Porcelain Figurine

The porcelain figurine grew waxen, her eyes grew glassy, shining as if alive, and with a sudden movement her arm dropped to her side, and timidly she turned her head to look around in wonderment. For years she had had her place upon the mantelpiece and now she tip-toed to its edge and gazed into the abyss of my living room—and then she turned to me and in a tiny voice she said, "You...you must be Hans Christian Andersen!"

"No, I am not," I answered.

"Oh!" she sort of sadly said, and slowly retraced her steps to that place where she had stood, assumed her familiar pose, and has retained it to this day.

Where Is That Part of Me?

Where is that part of me that writes long elaborate stories, writes line after line? No doubt that "personality" thinks that it deserves a vacation in the Caribbean and has departed, leaving me here for a while. Or perhaps it is in Canada, eating bacon and eggs by candlelight while the Eskimos patiently wait for him and impatient huskies howl. Yet does he loll perhaps in India, collecting prayer wheels and certain satins, green gauzes and yellow scarves ordinarily only treasured by primitive maidens and monks; now in some Himalayan hideaway he drinks dark tea surrounded by chests of ebony in which he keeps his collection of marbles, shining spheres of immortality; and does he not, though I be distant as in some dream, does he not ever think of me?

A Peculiar Greeting

"It is I, the rotten apple in the barrel, whose turn it is to fly and, smash and splatter, thrown like a meteorite from the hand of a master—ah! I have caught your eye—I greet you!"

Blue

Three violet flowers nod in the breeze, busying bees, ballooning their violent color in an ultraviolet fog around their pistils, tapering to cobalt.

A turquoise insect appears on a twig.

It vanishes into the blue sky.

"Would you like an orange?"

Bloody Indigo

The clouds at sunset scream bloody indigo, and the fox pisses on the pumpkin. In the orchard there is a thief in every tree. The black cat loves the scarecrow more than you or I might imagine. For them every night is Halloween.

The Bloodthirsty Macaw

The bloodthirsty macaw that killed raccoons spoke Dutch.

The Sky Darkened With Greenery

The plants began to move, first withdrawing their roots from the soil, they began to writhe on the ground, pounding the earth with their leaves, bucking and jumping, and finally waving, like wings, their leaves, they flew, fluttering but a few feet at first, but soon the brown ground was bare, and the sky darkened with greenery.

The Hangman

The hangman turned and shot the prisoner whom he had been about to hang, and then he hanged himself.

A Kitchen in Time

Grinding of grain, hour before dawn, room full of red light flickering, jumping shadows of oven light, the clang of cast iron, the cook speaks Chinese to his helpers who have pigtails, great frying pans hang from the ceiling, a jar of huge spoons stands on the table, through the hush of night a distant gong beats three times, franz, franz, franz...one senses this scene is occurring in a different century, that these words are being translated from a foreign language...perhaps from the German, around 1920 possibly in Prague, in a crowded tiny restaurant with checkered tablecloths a bank clerk is scribbling this on his lunch hour.

The What-you-might-call Madness

The what-you-might-call madness of a man who survived ten days without food at the bottom of an abandoned well was that from then on he developed a passion for climbing trees.

Michigan Highway Mirage

A Michigan highway...

Tired of walking, clothing full of sweat, handkerchief sopping wet, shoes dusty, and thirsty, thirsty—yearning for a true *mirage*.

Yearning for palm trees, a vivid lake that will vanish, or the sea that really recedes, even as we approach it.

Up ahead a gas station comes into view, and I hope the Coca-Cola will be cold...but what are those, moving into the driveway?

Camels...

Sky-blue Shadows

The speck of white that is a sailboat and the one that is a gull....

The speck of black that is the vulture and one on the waves way out there...a porpoise, perhaps, leading a parade underwater....

It is 8 a.m.

A gibbous moon rests quietly, goes almost unnoticed, in the cloudless sky. The shadows of the mountains on the moon are sky blue.

Freedom

"Freedom is spelled with seven letters," noticed the wise man, fondling his beard with his finger, thumbing its curls, while with his other hand he turned the pages of the Bhagavad Gita, and at that same moment that he said it, he opened the Book of Splendor, while with his other hand he made a note in pencil of a paragraph in the New Testament, while his other hand held up the Confucian Analects, and his other riffled the Koran, his other two hands are holding this book. He frowns.

"Bring me more light! Bring me my glasses!" he exclaims. "I have only two eyes, and I can hardly believe what I see here!"

A Saltwater Fish Tank

In the saloon in a great yacht, in an illuminated saltwater fish tank over the bar, there were fifty tropical fish, three scarlet squid, eight golden shrimp, and 48 snails.

In a furious storm, in which the ship floundered for five days, in the heart of the Pacific, it sank, a thousand miles from land, and it is said, and in a way it is true, in a sense, that there are no survivors.

Fire

Walking across the lawn in bare feet, otherwise rather nicely dressed for dinner, to turn around and see the building in flames, and to realize immediately that it is but a vision, understanding you must quickly leave this place you put on your shoes—and now to go in and face them all, old friends: to look into each face as if you had never seen it before, drunkenly making your adieus, probably we would think you weird, you who could receive the sign of our imminent doom.

Clouds of Orange

Clouds of orange dust rose into the air, and lightning shattered the sphere of summer silence with its thunder, smashing at the instant of the flame that tongued its way down the chimney filling the room with blazing death, utterly destroying the famous Oriental collection at the small museum deep in the suburbs of Chicago; and the fire would not be quenched by the downpour nor by Chicago firemen, but went on burning in the drizzle, so all that was standing was the ancient chimney—still smoking—when the Dalai Lama arrived.

Tell Us What the Tiger Fans Did *Then!*

"Tell us again, Grandpa...!" The retired baseball umpire sat deeper in his leather chair. The young boy continued, "How with the bases loaded in the ninth inning in the World Series the batter hit a line drive toward second base where you were standing and the ball hit you right between your arm and your chest and stuck there, and how your other hand just automatically reached over and plucked it from your armpit—"

King Midas

Her body flashes many bodies at me—lignum vitae, mercury, meerschaum, ice, jellyfish jade, banana-yellow cigarette smoke; she whispers hoarsely, "Think!—What would have happened had King Midas attained enlightenment?—Would that turn him into an ordinary human being?

"Or would the Universe turn into gold?"

Gumball

If You've never swallowed a gumball you won't know what I mean.

The Shoemaker

To be a shoemaker in a land where the people go predominantly barefoot is an art.

In Color

On moonless nights he walks over the oozy bog in snowshoes taking time exposures in color of luminous mushrooms. It is the police chief's son.

Recognition

He found a folded up foreign newspaper on the subway. He studied the front page trying to determine what language it was, but it was written in an unfamiliar alphabet. He was struck by the resemblance of someone pictured there to himself.

Memento

In a New England mansion after midnight, the great living room was lit by a few candles. Aware of distant voices, now alone in the room, now drunk, I sat on the floor clutching my glass.

As if having a race, a gang of baby Galapagos tortoises came galloping across the floor toward me; each was as big as a hatbox, and bore in blazing letters branded on its carapace the word "Memento."

The Sauce

The sauce was solid yellow ice, the fireplace was splattered, the cave cold, icicles hung from stalactites. A Neanderthal baby lay frozen in the arms of its mother, sprawled like a dancer since the days of the glaciers. Flashlights crisscrossed over the perfectly preserved bodies.

Lemon

He cut the lemon in half and found a hard-boiled egg inside.

Warts

A hook-and-ladder truck screeched a warning horn, and the horse-drawn wagon of apples and watermelon barely escaped collision. In pulling sharply to a halt, the wagon had swerved and a half-a-dozen apples fell onto the pavement right at the feet of a young boy who held a rope that was attached by a loop around the neck of a goat. The goat immediately began to eat one of the apples. The driver of the horse-and-wagon turned and stared at the goat eating the apple, and at the apples on the ground, and to the young boy he said thoughtfully, "I suppose it doesn't really matter, seeing as we're just characters in a story."

The boy said, "Imagine all my freckles turned into warts."

The Collector of Cymbals

He built his house over the elevator shaft of an abandoned salt mine, and in his house there was a small room whose only window was a trap door in the floor. He was a collector of cymbals, and whenever he got hold of a cymbal he would drop it down the shaft, and listen to it echo as it fell. He was a writer, like me.

Objects of Mu

Objects of Mu, pearls of Ur in turquoise pools repose, while bold ghouls, six bald heads whose doctorates were on the dead, archeologists, gaze fondly down on them, their "discovery" (six grins above the blue bowl) untouched beneath the temple for six thousand years, each still perfection of pale purity. On being popped into a felt cloth the finest pearl reflects—"How different were the smiles of the ancient kings."

Five Hundred Yellow Cabs

The intersection filled with yellow cabs.

The garage of the cab company was on fire and the news had flitted from taxi radio to radio and cabs came from all over the city out of curiosity and, like bewildered insects whose nest had been destroyed, they gathered and moved around the huge burning building, blocking the way of fire trucks, some vehicles abandoned in the middle of the street as drivers got out and gathered in groups to chat where they could get a better view, and as two floors collapsed with a tremendous crash and fire filled the windows with renewed fury and the black smoke of grease and gasoline put a plume into the stratosphere, the drivers began to blow their horns as cab drivers under stress have a wont to do, and that mourning music, such vibrant brass, of five hundred taxi drivers blowing their horns could be heard across the river.

On the New

Winging past floods down into Ethiopia, the stork disappeared over the horizon, while far below by a pyramid a Nile sparrow sang for a dying Pharaoh.

His tents were like flames on the desert sand.

Tethered white horses flashed in the sunlight.

Far below in the inner folds of the cloth palace a cricket hailed the sparrow by his own song, and together they sang.

The wind joined them, playing the palms of the oasis, and the tent posts creaked, shifting from foot to foot as if tents thought of dancing this morning.

The new pyramid had already begun to practice its silence.

Text
of
There Are Different Kinds of Writing
A Shorter Version

THE ORIGINAL *THERE ARE DIFFERENT KINDS OF WRITING* IS AN
EVENING-LENGTH PROSE WORK, USING MICROTONAL MUSIC
FOR THE BASS RECORDER (PART I)
AND FOR THE FAMILY OF RECORDERS (PART II)

BY

TUI ST GEORGE TUCKER

*   *

The dumbest guy I have ever met was an editor.

There is one thing about editors—they are idealists: there has never been an editor who would not rather have written a great novel or a great poem than do the job he is doing. In their own eyes they are failures.

But this particular editor had developed cancer of the tongue when he was ten, and his tongue had been removed surgically. The operation was successful, and the disease did not recur. However, for the rest of his life he was unable to speak, other than those certain words which can be pronounced without opening the mouth. He breathed through his nose when he spoke.

When he wanted to say "yes," he said—Uh-hunh.

When he wanted to say "no," he said—Unh-unh.

When he didn't understand, he would say—Hunh?

When he was thinking something over he would say—Hmm....

*   *

That a man could sit there feeling anxiety, breathing shallowly, moving his toes inside his shoes, swallowing, licking his lips, raising his eyebrows and then frowning, sighing sadly, twisting in his chair, reaching for a magazine and then letting it drop to the floor without picking it up...that a writer could sit there doing really nothing...contemplating a far-off editor who might at that moment be reading his manuscript, instead of *herself* writing what could have been...what, good God, might have been a great novel!

Hmm!

*   *

Scrunched into the chair, her arm falling asleep, her black hair billowing over the purple pillow, wearing yellow film, perhaps taffeta, a white shoe askew on the bedpost, drunk. Steadily the ocean breeze rushes through the jalousies.

Costa Rica!

*   *

I am serious as the dead.

Some find the dead grotesque, but the dead see your lively exertions, in the face of the future, as grotesque.

*   *

Noticeably now, if there were but attention, if that activity might be envisioned, could it but be conceived—were I to invent it for the moment and place it there on the table like a model, so that the idea could be got, bursting on the brain in a fever of work—would you recognize it if you saw it?

*   *

If I could ride around a bit, sitting in the back seat of a great car, perhaps gliding through the yellow countryside of Ohio in the afternoon on a fine Fall day, or zooming through the midnight black of a New England Summer night with the rain beating down, drops dancing on the highway in the headlights, or picking our way on a Spring day around Baltimore streets passing among glad throngs, through the racket of everyday, moving ponderously, our dark brown Cadillac purrs, and is stared at by children.

*   *

Arid land, black banks of dust, where hills change places daily and the wind is long, the dirty dunes rising in hot clouds to cake with grime the gristle left of yesterday's lamb that the wanderer eats. Tomorrow he shall chew his belt, the next day his tongue. It is Arthur Rimbaud!

*   *

And here I am at the grave of Yeats and it's midnight. My horse is miserable. There's a full moon somewhere but it's black, black blanketing rain that greets the visitor from America.

*   *

In a far-flung corner of the Third World the fur flag of the Alaskan nationalists blew off the flagpole and was chased by three wolves across an airstrip, delaying the take-off of the small black plane containing three snowblind East German spies, whose fate it is to be sent back here, and to be eaten by polar bears.

*   *

The fire hose was tied into a dozen knots. The blaze consumed the building that was so hated by its tenants. The landlord collected the full insurance. Two people died in it. Its light cast flickering shadows a block away. Passengers taking the air on the deck of the Staten Island Ferry all noted the conflagration, and commented upon it.

*   *

Once upon a time a fox bit a furrier who was fishing on a private lake in Pennsylvania. The lake belongs to the fox.

*   *

Holding cupped in his hands three pieces of dry ice insulated by green napkins, the invisible man set them afloat atop the tropical fish-tank pool, like three smoking bars of bubbling soap.

A gramophone was playing a onetime top tune on the Hit Parade.

A lemon fell onto the rug with such momentum it rolled out into the middle of the room, and it will remain there, unpicked-up, untouched for at least fifteen minutes after this story is forgotten.

The man, whose hand was seen with green napkins dropping dry ice, now appeared above the water and rose to his feet from where he'd been kneeling behind the long empty fishpool.

A voice at the door exclaimed, "Pick up that lemon *immediately!*"

*   *

Crockery, cookery—shard, to be sure, but still with the taint of ancient oil, attracts the hordes of cockroach ghosts to the archeological site, affording to the few, those sensitives for whom the dead live, ghastly sensations.

*   *

Worm-eaten, moth-eaten, the cocoon that was left on fulfilling its metamorphosis by the famous *Phantom Moth-of-Gold* fell into the hands, by luck, of the incredible weaver who lived on the equator in Ecuador nine hundred years ago, who unspun its strong, invisible thread upon a bone spool decorated by an emerald, put the spool into a box-of-spools intended for use in the future, and on that very day was buried by his god, the volcano, under a thin layer of lava.

*   *

He placed it there with a thud.

Then he quickly covered its lip with melted beeswax and put a blue-clay stopper on the huge jar, and covered it in the deep hole with earth, mumbling prayers in a tongue that no one speaks now, in a language dead two thousand years. Stamping the earth firm over the grave, he tried to think of the future, much as you or I might think of the future—imagining someone coming across this page two thousand years hence, but nobody understanding the language.

Thud.

*   *

Look at that building framed by the mist, there is purple light inside it.

There are thirteen golden men inside it, their eyes closed.

Patiently they wait for us, for years they have been dreaming that it is us approaching through the wet grass.

*   *

An unoiled wagon sang a song, some Oriental mountain melody that plain folk in Kansas cannot appreciate; but the whining of the wheel is the whistling of a god, a Buddha no bigger than an elf that sits six inches high between the ears of a horse heading for a house where a baby will be born. The baby will be the reincarnation of so-and-so (I would not dare to try to pronounce that name).

For centuries upon centuries it has been the duty of this immortal, magnificent, miniature Buddha to attend each rebirth of so-and-so.

It is his first visit to America.

*   *

"He brought me a bouquet of whirlpools and tornadoes and I put them in this cracked vase."

Where precipices lunge, chasms fall: mountains lounge, then avalanche.

*   *

"It was the person next to me.

"I tell you, it was that person next to me!

"I was reading this book aloud, and there was a person sitting here beside me listening, and it was that person who did it, not me.

"I was just sitting here reading this book aloud, and my eyes were on the page, and I didn't even realize that my listener had vanished. I tell you, I don't know which way that person went!"

The Getaway Car

In the darkest hours of the night on the country road which passes the county prison, the jailed and the jailers alike can sometimes hear a ghastly cranking, as if a ghost were cranking a ghostly Model-T Ford; then they hear the motor start, backfire several times, and then depart; and as prisoners and guards alike are listening to the chugging of the motor fading out in the distance down the road, the fleeing ghost utters its cry: Ah-GOO-gah! Ah-GOO-gah!

Mona Lisa Meets Buddha

Up in heaven the curtains fluttered, the curtains fluttered, the curtains fluttered, and the Mona Lisa entered at one end of a small hall, which was hung with many veils.

Up in heaven the curtains fluttered, fluttered, fluttered, and the Buddha entered the hall at the other end.

They smiled.

The Hidden Ballroom at Versailles

Elegant and opulent, yet undiscovered, "the hidden ballroom" at Versailles, whose entire floor is made with many fragile panes into a smooth, single surface of mirror, rests undusty in darkness, unentered for two centuries by a flicker, nary a moonbeam nor match, lamp, nor any light, except for one time. Then, a tiny batch of insect eggs (blown through a crevice down through an imperfection in the molding onto the great glass floor) hatched fireflies.

That was in 1893.

Nineteen Paragraphs

A Chocolate Reptile
& 3 untitled paragraphs

The deep-brown carnivorous mushroom with a cap shaped like a doughnut swallowed through the hole a tiny green chameleon tail first, and the last of it to disappear was the pink revealed by its extended jaws emitting an ultrasonic scream as it vibrated a forked carnelian tongue. No human could have heard that scream—one hundred million years ago—yet it was immediately heard by a mother, by an eighty-five-foot-long green chameleon, who twisted her neck around to that place on the ground where the murderous mushroom grew, and she bit off its bitter cap, letting the foul fungus fall to the forest floor, and from the wound the chocolate-colored baby reptile scampered free.

*

The sacred, flowery orange ceremonial robe of the Dowager Empress was sold in London at auction at Christie's to a dirty old man for cash. But he was not a filthy-rich American; he was an Australian impostor, the money counterfeit—and the old varmint vanished. The robe turned up two years later in the boudoir of a murdered English actress in Brisbane. Although the garment is undamaged, she had had it altered.

*

The orchid opened like a firecracker, all at once—with a silent explosion of odor that struck like a gong in the jungle gloom, with a stench so strong it seared the nostrils of mammals of every size and species, from jungle mouse to jaguar that were within twenty yards of the gaping blossom, inducing in all of them symptoms of extreme seasickness. It is the only flower fertilized by snakes.

*

The old French king had his dentist construct for his aging mistress a set of false teeth with thirty-six real pearls, perfectly matched, put in place of the teeth. Although her bite was perfect, pearls are fragile, and the only time she used them to eat was when she ate oysters. When she wore her pearls in public, she couldn't help but smile.

Frenzy of Barbarians
& 7 untitled paragraphs

Where grass grows nine feet tall and tablecloths of beige moss spread out on every boulder, and utensils, delicately carved by doodling nature from the bones of vultures, lie exposed on the brown rocks to dry out noon after noon undisturbed on the impenetrable plain; for the great grass grows densely about each boulder, and the bending blades that gently dip are razor sharp and in the gales of autumn can cut birds in half as they wildly thrash, in that wondrous wind like a Paris of Fencers with sabers delirious, all slashing—then like a Frenzy of Barbarians—annually they cut each other down.

*

When Lincoln fell, how the Arabians wept. On the White House steps a clump of women wailed—in the conventional way—behind pastel veils. A saffron coach stood darkly by, its four black stallions, such startling beasts in beauty, trembled impatiently and were calmed by strange words from turbaned, stately servants, while for hours the women kept the vigil. With a curving four-foot blade in each hand, twin giants in pantaloons stood guarding them, arms akimbo. The curious sensed that they did not speak English, and no one questioned them.

*

He sold his seal hole and his igloo to the bank for quite a sizable sum, indeed, for oil had been disovered offshore. And so the old Eskimo hunter went to Florida to live out his remaining years. He loved the weather, and practically lived on the beach, and could be found there on every day of the year. Though admittedly, his favorites were those freezing days which Florida experiences every year, days which drive disconsolate tourists indoors, and at these times he had the beach completely to himself. For the one thing about civilization that he could never get used to was being surrounded by crowds of people. He was affable and affluent and soon made many friends, yet often when they or the crush of the throngs on the beach overwhelmed him, he would take out his kayak and his spear, the only possessions he had brought South from the Far North, and he would point his boat toward the horizon. He would be out there several days, sometimes in the foulest storms.

He would visit uninhabited mangrove keys, and fish.

*

The meadow that stretches among strangely shaped lakes, where swans are, and buffalo meander among great green boulders—there is an ordinary giraffe with its family of albinos!—ostriches; slow armadillos sunning themselves in large groups; large land turtles abound; although there are many strange snakes, none are dangerous; many kinds of grazing beasts with intricately shaped horns; elephants. There is another plain on which all the animals are carnivorous.

*

The sleepwalker strangely snapped his fingers, causing the dog to bark, startling a burglar who had been about to enter the house, who changed his mind and left the premises. The dog went back to sleep. The walker awoke in the morning to find himself in his favorite comfortable chair.

*

The French milliner and the seamstress were roommates and had a lifelong association in a shop below their living quarters on the Rue Armboussent. Their dog was named Renée and their white cat was named Celine. Both animals were deaf. The animals were thoroughbreds. The dog was a tiny Mexican Hairless Chihuahua, and the cat was a gorgeous Angora, a long-haired tom with blue eyes.

*

If there is nothing to wrap up, nothing to bring to a close, no farfetched tales that turn out to be dreams, no light on the hill as a signal, and if there are nothing but fragments between commas, and if adjectives are not quite right, if hammers are silent though not still...still, thank god I don't have a tin ear. *(After Virginia Woolf)*

*

(For V. W.) She set out to make herself into a monster with a will with a well-thought-out pill of dried particles of pickled porkfat, gold and sandalwood, rose thorns and crushed thrush beaks, fresh shavings from balsa knots, or sawdust from the core of a living redwood, unused shot from a Puritan's musket, and the tips of trout fins, flaming arbutus roots and dried Scotch whiskey scratched from a varnished desk, ten white warts from a pretzel, ten O!'s from a page in the Iliad, ten tips clipped from French swords, and from an astronomical map—the Pleiades cut apart from each other, half-a-dozen motes captured from the air on a sunny day, one sixteenth of a teaspoon

(more)

Fear of Firecrackers
& 6 untitled paragraphs

Rain filled the flat plate which inadvertently had been left all night in the yard, and in the early morning sunlight it was visited by birds, by a robin, some purple finches and starlings. On the previous evening a hole had been dug there as a grave for the cat who had been seventeen years old on the Fourth of July. The cat had been born on that holiday and had carried with him a lifelong fear of firecrackers and had retreated under the porch to die on his birthday.

*

A tramp steamer carried a full load of used rubber tires from South Asia to Puget Sound. The ship was permeated with the odor of used tires. Even the ice cubes from the refrigerator in the galley smelled like rubber. In the middle of the placid Pacific the long churning wake of the ship smelled like a busy highway.

*

At the summit of a mountain in Chile a luminous gnat landed at night near the center of the giant lens of the largest telescope in the world, laid its luminous eggs there, and then vanished into the heavens.

*

He held a newspaper over his head in the sudden downpour, and yet it soon was sopping wet, and disintegrated in his hands, leaving a word from a large headline plastered on his bald spot.

*

Looking like a piece of the moon, a giant clinker from an abandoned coal furnace is found by a five-year-old with his nine-year-old brother, who are playing among the ruined buildings of the old factory down by the river. The only intact structure on the grounds is a brick chimney four stories high. Goldenrod grows between the railroad tracks.

*

Conversation was difficult but irrepressible among the dozen patients in the doctor's waiting room, who were all ages and from all walks of life, there alike to be treated for severe hiccups.

*

It is his lifework to meticulously draw with a diamond-tipped pencil great arrays of streaming raindrops on panes of perfect glass.

Prose for Dancing

For Nannette Domingos

To have a good cat is a good beginning.
My typewriter is a *Meower.*

*

Beauty mused, as if to herself, "When I agreed to be in this piece it was understood that there was to be a fresh typewriter ribbon."

*

The flies are chasing the mosquitoes, so the unanswering centuries I address are not entirely silent.

*

The bubbling Babylonian tablet came clean in the bath of acid.

*

He was a trader in tourmaline, emerald, and ruby in the back bush; and he wore baggy trousers, each leg of which had twenty pockets; and each pocket had a button, and each held a gem.
He had his legs memorized.

*

The shadow of a maple tree encroached upon the cat, whose pupils widen....
The breeze dealt him a shadow blow; he turns one ear.
A butterfly distracted him, and he turns his head to follow its flight.
But now a garter snake skims over the grass, and when it arrives at a point about two feet in front of the cat, the snake stops, and raises its head until its eyes are level with the cat's. It sways gently to and fro, and its forked tongue shoots in and out. It is as if the forces of evolution had all conspired to create the snake to act just so in order to astonish a curious cat.
But in confronting all of the forces of nature incarnate in the moving body of the snake, a black cat can have recourse to the

occult. With an expressive smile the black cat crossed his legs and took off his white socks.

*

His job was to take the gum from the bottom of the seats at the movie theater.

She was an usherette.

*

The hatch hung open, and the waves washed in, putting a blanket of sand on the bottom of the boat.

*

An orange flag swirling in a stiff breeze ballooned out and engulfed the figure of the general, who, in trying to untangle himself, fell off the reviewing stand at the parade of the paratroopers.

*

He was the Emperor of Antarctica.

He was the dominant male in the colony of emperor penguins that meet to breed on the Ross Ice Shelf.

He was the Emperor of emperors.

*

The Jostlers are an ugly club whose sole activity is to create confusion in crowds, riots at rock concerts, and mass hysteria and mayhem at sporting events.

*

The nimble nincompoop would adroitly climb up any streetlamp in the park and stand on his head atop the globe, bathed in light.

*

When I grumble, only the volcano listens. When the volcano grumbles, everybody listens.

People would be crazy not to listen to a volcano. A man who talks to a volcano is crazy.

*

The ibex stretched its neck upward while standing on the rims of its hoofs.

The ibis stretched its neck upward while standing on the tips of its toes on one foot.

Why should there be such an art as the one I practice?

*

A piece of English rag, a tube of French maroon, a sable brush...do you get the picture?

*

I filled my boots with marbles and ran home barefoot through a thundershower.

*

I found a ladies' wristwatch in my tuna fish sandwich.

*

He stole a blanket from a polo pony and raced diagonally across the playing field

*

I am stuck in this chair in front of my typewriter like a fly on flypaper.

*

I'm beginning to see the light that's coming in through the back of my head, since recently I started getting bald.

*

The choirboys sneezed in unison when the assistant conductor raised his baton.

*

She coughed into her sandwich, and a piece of lettuce from it fell into the goldfish pond.

*

The yellow flame rose into the air like a yellow rose about a yard wide.

*

She walked on stilts through the field of sunflowers.

*

A silhouette of a white cat appeared on the window ledge beside the black geranium.

*

He manufactured horses for merry-go-rounds, and spent his paycheck each Sunday at the racetrack.

*

The ceiling of the cellar dripped slime.
The floor was covered with broken slate.
The only door in the room opened into the bottom of a well. A ladder of iron spikes protruding from the well wall allowed a climber easy access.
All that was needed was a fire in the grate to make it a cozy place.

*

She had twenty thousand pairs of green galoshes all the same size, which she bought off a boat from Hong Kong because they just fit.

*

LOT BOTANY
A Picture Book of Weeds,
Including Certain Wildflowers and Small Trees
Commonly Found in City Vacant Lots
Or Growing beside Fences of Gas Stations and Parking Lots,
Which Spring Up, Survive, Thrive and Spread
Unattended by Man.

*

"Miniature flamingos live upon our bayou, and now at sunset will skim the surface feasting on the schools of singing flying fish. Would you like to take a walk to the end of the pier!"

"Not especially."

Brilliant Silence

Two Alaskan Kodiak bears joined a small circus, where the pair appeared in a nightly parade pulling a covered wagon. The two were taught to somersault, to spin, to stand on their heads, and to dance on their hind legs, paw in paw, stepping in unison. Under a spotlight the dancing bears, a male and a female, soon became favorites of the crowd. The circus went south on a west coast tour through Canada to California and on down into Mexico, through Panama into South America, down the Andes the length of Chile to those southernmost isles of Tierra del Fuego.

There a jaguar jumped the juggler, the owner of the circus, and afterward mortally mauled the animal trainer, and the shocked showpeople disbanded in dismay and horror. In the confusion the bears went their own way. Without a master, they wandered off by themselves into the wilderness on those densely wooded, wildly windy, subantarctic islands. Utterly away from people, on an out-of-the-way uninhabited island, and in a climate they found ideal, the bears mated, thrived, multiplied, and after a number of generations populated the entire island. Indeed, after some years, descendants of the two moved out onto half a dozen adjacent islands; and seventy years later, when scientists finally found and enthusiastically studied the bears, it was discovered that all of them, to a bear, were performing splendid circus tricks.

On nights when the sky is bright and the moon is full, they gather to dance. They gather the cubs and the juveniles in a circle around them. They gather together out of the wind at the center of a sparkling, circular crater left by a meteorite which had fallen in a bed of chalk. Its glassy walls are chalk white, its flat floor is covered with white gravel, and it is well drained and dry. No vegetation grows within. When the moon rises above it, the light reflecting off the walls fills the crater with a pool of moonlight, so that it is twice as bright on the crater floor as anywhere else in that vicinity. Scientists speculate that originally the full moon had reminded the two bears of the circus spotlight, and for that reason they danced. Yet, it might be asked, what music do the descendants dance to?

Paw in paw, stepping in unison...what music can they possibly hear inside their heads as they dance under the full moon and the Aurora Australis, as they dance in brilliant silence?

The Largest Wave in the World

A hurricane sent the 200-foot radio tower dancing upright across the fields, its guide wires trailing giant blue sparks.

The suspension bridge split lengthwise down the middle. Each side of the highway was suspended by vertical strands to its single cable, and though the two great cables stayed firmly fixed to the towers, the two pieces of highway broke loose and were pushed mightily away from the towers and flapped horrendously in the great winds. Built of massive blocks of stone and steel sunk deep into bedrock, the bridge towers held firmly to the ground, but the tops of the towers began to vibrate like two buzzers, or more precisely: as the towers were sunk into a single great piece of stone, and as the towers themselves were perfect geometric replicas of each other, the bridge towers buzzed *in phase* like the prongs of a tuning fork, producing a single pure tone. For fifteen minutes while the eye of the storm passed overhead, the buzzing resonated inside that giant cylinder of still air, and a strange musical tone was heard around the world.

Every seismograph jammed, and it's judged that it was the loudest continuous sound heard on earth during the time since life began.

In the base of the bridge tower, deep inside, were a number of rooms where a hundred people huddled in more or less comfort, safe from the holocaustal winds. As the eye of the storm passed overhead, and as the wind suddenly died down to an uncanny dead calm, those people ventured outside to look around in wonderment. This is the largest suspension bridge ever built, and it is located on the Eastern coast of the United States, crossing the Hudson River at The Narrows, just before that river empties into the Atlantic Ocean. When those hundred people came outside onto a broad stone terrace, they looked out toward the nearby ocean and saw the sea hugely tossing though there was not a breath of wind, and they noticed an odd silence.

Some shouted at the top of their lungs and one raised a wooden chair in the air and crashed it to the floor, but those activities made not the slightest sound.

For the strange musical tone had "jammed" their ears, just as it jammed the seismographs. Their ears temporarily had stopped functioning. They were utterly deaf. Later they all said they could hear the mysterious musical note, not with their ears but with every cell in their bodies.

After several minutes had passed, they noticed that the waters of the ocean were receding. Where a moment before the waters had been hugely tossing, it was now dry land, and that place where the water met the land now seemed several miles away. The thick billows of clouds of the hurricane wall rose thirty thousand feet into the early evening sky and came down to a hundred feet above the surface of the ocean; the ceiling of clouds remained in place as the level of the ocean fell, so soon they bad a view—beneath the storm—of the floor of the ocean, which was now dry land as far as they could see, and they say they saw before them a fantastic canyon cut into the floor of the ocean, which in the distance got deeper and deeper as well as wider: and they say they saw far off between the walls of the canyon a brilliant orange moon, they insist *they saw the moonrise,* that it bathed them in orange light, that the canyon floor and the bridge were bathed in orange light. And that it took several minutes before the glowing moon slipped up behind that whirling wall of cloud that by then was fast approaching. In sudden pitch darkness and wind they scrambled into the rooms at the base of the tower, and locked the doors tight.

And every one of those hundred survived it, the wave.

Orange

Though a man may be white from frostbite, purple with rage, yellow from jaundice, green while seasick, green with envy, in redfaced apoplexy, turned black by the sea when drowned, or browned by the sun, now gray in horror, or in the pink for pleasure, yet I know of no case that a man may be orange.

Though the villain is black, the coward yellow and the novice green, I know nothing of the character of that man who is orange.

The human body's fluids, organs and flesh can be found to be of every hue, except that there is no organ, liquid, muscle nor piece of fat that is pure orange.

Excepting orange, in death we may meet every shade.

There is no word that rhymes with orange.

2

Orange is the best color.

Where this color is present, gloom requires effort.

Good spirits are created in this light.

With fixed, triangular eyes, a jack-o'-lantern stares at me, but in vain tries to raise his eyebrows at my thought.

Whatever the candle in the pumpkin sees, it illuminates.

Among great lights he holds his candle, and his grin is not discouraged by the white glare; nor later on the windowsill is he disconsolate at viewing the great dark, outside.

By his light children are transformed into—Good Lord! into what!?...(there go a pirate and rabbit walking hand-in-hand with Death)...perhaps, into gods this evening, hallowed, mellowed by orange.

I have asked myself seriously, "Why do the young stare so seriously upon the face of the pumpkin?"

As, even now, I conjure an image of that hideous visage, yet benign, so orange, I wonder—who in history's name could you have been? What life did a body lead to be left so headless?

I have tried to imagine the body of the jack-o'-lantern.

"Are you John the Baptist?"

"No," answers the pumpkin.

"Are you Marie Antoinette?"

"No."

"Are you that Greek whose body the women tore apart, whose head they left in a cave, where it alone survived and prophesied, and then allegedly was lost—are you that head, priest of poetry and music, Orpheus, himself? Is this what you've come to?"

The pumpkin is silent.

Perhaps he is embarrassed because of his teeth, or contemplates the bittersweet.

3

The New York City garbage barge was called the *Ornery Henry* and its sister ship the *Frankincense*. The city sold the second-hand boats to an African company, and they were tightly tied together, side by side, and towed—bound for Africa, into the eastern Atlantic into the vicinity of the Canary Islands, where they encountered a hurricane. Such was the fury of the storm, the barges were cut loose at sea, and abandoned. For several years they drifted—still securely lashed together—southward, and then westward, caught up in the North Equatorial Current drifting inexorably west toward a line of islands that extends several hundred miles off the coast of Venezuela. Many of these are small islands without fresh water, are uninhabited, remote and unvisited; and it was on high ground at the center of one of them that another great storm deposited the boats. The garbage barges are now empty, clean and spotless, bone dry and sitting in the sand, without a speck of paint, silver gray, bleached by tropical sun and repeatedly washed by the afternoon rains and blown dry by a ceaseless, salty warm wind. A simple one-room cabin had been built at the back of one of the barges, and its door had been wrenched from its hinges long ago by the wind off the Canary Islands. A brilliant and large, intensely rusty hinge was still attached to the cabin doorway, a slender triangle pointed outward like a stiffened pennant, bright as a flag.

"You mean it is an orange door-hinge?"

"It is an orange door-hinge."

Another Impostor

Once upon a time a millionaire playboy burned his face off in an automobile accident.

After that he became a recluse, he stopped seeing all his friends, and he lived up in his big stone house on large grounds which he never left.

Wild rumors ran about him, about the splendor of his life, about rare wines he drank, and women, women were there, it was whispered, and they said he had great collections of things like art and books and drums and daggers, and they said he kept live smooth fish in his secret swimming pool someplace deep within the walls of his impenetrable house.

His theater was on the roof, and he'd hire whole Broadway casts to play for him there, and stars of the ballet and concert stage to come and perform for him.

He never spoke to any of the stars who came into his house, but they would see him occasionally over the footlights with a black covering over his face, languidly lounging in his comfortable chair, the only chair in the theater, smoking a cigar or, perhaps, with a purple drink.

The millionaire spoke to no one.

His go-between with the world was his butler, who paid his bills, arranged his entertainments, and was interviewed by the press, and who, because of his peculiar relationship to the millionaire, also became famous.

One day an actor who was feeling very depressed because he had no work was sitting in the Waldorf Cafeteria reading a newspaper.

He happened to read a story about the eccentric millionaire and he realized—he was about the same height and build as this millionaire, and he was about the same age—and he realized that if he could somehow kill the millionaire and take his place, why, it would be easy to impersonate this man who spoke to no one and wore a black covering over his face.

He was afraid of the butler, though.

So he studied, from newspaper files and things, the habits and characteristics of the butler and the millionaire.

One dark night he sneaked onto the grounds and by luck ran into the millionaire, who was looking down an old well at the back of the house.

And so he hit the millionaire over the head and killed him.

It was dark by the well. He hurriedly got into the millionaire's clothes and put the black covering over his face and dumped the millionaire's body into the well, and he noticed at the time that the body didn't make a splash.

So dressed, the impostor walked into the house, and into a life of ease and luxury.

And he found it was a cinch!

Because this butler was—a perfect butler.

He never had to give an order. The butler just knew what to do. The butler would bring him his breakfast, would run his bath, he arranged for him to have women, furnished him with cigarettes of hashish, ran the household, and planned all his fabulous entertainments.

His living was effortless.

And after a while he realized—no one could ever discover his identity. The scheme was perfect.

And he was right.

No one would ever discover his identity.

But this man's weakness was his conceit. You see, it never occurred to him that someone else might get the same idea he got. It never occurred to him that the man he killed was not the millionaire at all, but was an impostor, like himself, and that in a couple of months another impostor would come along and kill him, and that as a matter of fact, during the last few years there had been quite a few impostors, each with the same weakness, that same conceit.

No, no one ever knew of this—except the butler, of course—but he never told, because he likes his job.

The Cat Who Owned an Apartment

Once upon a time a man sat listening to music.

His fingers hung limply over the arms of his chair, his eyes drooped, and his feet rested on a sheepskin-covered ottoman. He breathed shallowly.

An expensive phonograph was twirling in the corner; a booming symphony filled the room, and filled the universe as far as he was concerned, so passionate was his attention. Each note he heard, each quiver of the harp strings, bang of the cymbals, nuance of the violin, snore of the tuba, plink of the piano.

The man loved music. He was a connoisseur.

His Siamese cat sat on the table.

The cat heard the music.

But the cat heard other things too. It heard the honking of automobiles, the sound of the refrigerator, leaves stirring in the wind, a dog barking down the street, someone shout.

The man heard none of this. He was completely absorbed in the music.

Then the cat heard the sound of the window being slowly opened and the floor creaking as a man in a leather jacket, wearing tennis shoes, stepped through.

But the man listening to music heard none of this.

The cat heard the sound of the man's tennis shoes as he tiptoed across the room, and the sound of a knife being drawn from the leather jacket.

The cat yawned and listened to the sound of the knife as it sank into his master's throat, his master's gasp, and to the sound of the man who was listening to music as he rolled down to the floor—dead.

The cat listened to the murderer as he walked back toward the open window, and heard him climb out onto the fire escape.

Then there was the sound of footsteps in the alleyway three stories below.

The light from the open window shone on the murderer. He jumped off the fire escape onto a wooden ledge which ran along the building.

The cat heard all this. But the cat heard the ledge creak as well. The murderer listened intently to the footsteps.

And the cat heard the ledge creaking and creaking and finally breaking, and heard the scream of the murderer as he fell to his death on the pavement below, and the shriek of the child who'd been passing.

Then the cat heard a funny little scratching noise behind the refrigerator.

A mouse poked his head out, pricked his ears, sniffed, and scampered across the room.

The cat leaped.

He landed on the mouse, and bit.

The mouse was dead. The cat looked around. They were all dead. It was his apartment now.

10,000 Reflections

A hundred feet up in the air, the great crystal chandelier was flashing with the light of five hundred candles nestled in its glass.

Five hundred flames tossing, reflected ten thousand times.

The rude guests were aghast at the glittering giant—for the hall below was filled with peasants—it is 1789, it is July 14, the French Revolution is on!

This is the great dining hall of the Duke, his dinner guests have been stabbed in their chairs, and while their corpses sit still at their table, the peasants eat—grabbing fistfuls of cake—gobbling it.

As the dining hall filled with the riffraff, ravenous, as it became chock-full with hysterical murderers—all waving blades and clubs and shrieking with freedom and passion—the great chandelier began to tinkle.

Now it is an awesome sound to hear ten thousand finely cut pieces of crystal begin to rub shoulders, and the acoustics in the room were good.

It was as if someone had begun to ring a million glass bells all at once.

The tinkle cut through every shriek.

The sweating throng grew quiet.

All eyes fastened themselves in wonder on the thing, all faces were turned up, aghast at the trembling splendor, and to a man— terror struck.

It was almost imperceptible at first—the sound of deep sighs in the silence around the tinkling; just as imperceptibly the chandelier had begun—this way and that, back and forth, on the cast-iron chain on which it hung—the chandelier began to swing.

The room became filled with the sound of sighs as they all saw it moving in the arc of the pendulum.

Then the sighs ceased.

The pendulum swung—it swung faster now, each time its arc grew wider, its five hundred flames were bent flat, first this way, then that, as it raced through the air, increasing its speed.

The nature of the tinkle changed: in gaining momentum the tinkling grows silent as the chandelier plunges on its path, but on the end of each swing the tinkle returns, a crescendo of glass, a hundred times louder!

But in the silence of the swing a tiny voice can now be heard.

It is the tiny sound of sobbing, of wanton weeping, it is the tiny voice of Grief.

It is the voice of an angel, and it seems to come from the very center of the air above their heads.

Every member of the mob is a statue, face upturned, eyes closed, breathing deeply in perfect time with the swinging light, hypnotized.

Here is a perfect example of mass hypnosis. They are all unconscious, deeply asleep.

They'll stand here like this until the sunlight wakens them at dawn, but their memories will be all confused, and they'll never have any idea what was happening on this night; they hear no tears, nor how the childish shriek of grief turns into the rage of revenge in each crescendo.

The pendulum swings faster.

The room suddenly darkens as most of the candles blow out, and on the next swing the room was plunged into a pitch blackness, utterly lightless, and at that moment the five-year-old daughter of the Duke lost her grip on the cast-iron chain of the chandelier, which feverishly she had been pumping as yesterday she had her playground swing, and her grief-shaken body flew through the air, from the dead light was flung, through the blackness, pitched over their heads.

The Prime Minister's Grandfather

A walrus swallowed a candle, grimaced, made a little face at the taste and decided it was a mackerel, and then dove to the bottom of the Bering Sea, nosing about among cold boulders where the best lobster live. He chose to glide about a foot above a seaweed meadow over beside a new Canadian submarine being shown off by the Canadian Secretary of the Navy, who was playing host to several members of Parliament, and the Prime Minister, himself, on an inspection tour.

"Mr. Prime Minister," said the captain eagerly, "you asked whether we might see some underwater life, and I think this meadow might be a good place."

And he gave crisp orders that powerful lights located on the outside of the submarine be switched on, so that when the periscope was dropped beneath the surface of the water, it was possible to view the bed of waving weeds for several hundred yards in any direction, such is the clarity there of those northern waters, such the penetrating power of modern submarine lights.

"This was an expensive ship," mused the head of state, and as if to test its mettle he rapped the wall three times with his cane.

On the other side of the two-inch steel-plate wall was the walrus who was worrying a steel loop that swung loosely on a hinge, used to secure the submarine with cable when the boat was at a dock.

Mimicking the Minister's knock with mammalian fidelity, the walrus knocked the steel loop against the ship's hull three times.

"That noise came from outside," said the captain.

The Prime Minister rapped twice against the wall with his cane, and the walrus, obviously enjoying the game, rapped back—twice.

"Who is out there?" asked the Prime Minister.

"It's odd. I don't see a living thing out there," said the captain, turning the periscope this way and that. Fish were often curious about the submarine, but today the presence of the walrus had caused them all to flee, and the walrus at the moment was swimming about directly above the periscope, his attention attracted by its turning, but he was out of view.

"May I look?" inquired the Prime Minister, and he put his eye to the glass, and at that moment the walrus swam down so that his face filled the field of the periscope's view.

"Good Christ, it's my grandfather!" whispered the Prime Minister, aghast and visibly shaken. As a boy of nine he had attended his grandfather's funeral in Toronto, and lately the old man had appeared several times in his dreams, admonishing him to conduct the affairs of state in a proper fashion. *"You protect the wild animals..."* his grandfather had said to him in his dream only last night. The old man had wagged his finger at him and in his dream he had felt like a child. *"The walrus, the musk ox, the caribou, the polar bear, the white fox..."* The Prime Minister had awoken in a cold sweat and had clutched his heart with a pang of guilt.

On disembarking from the submarine at the naval base, the Prime Minister got on the phone to the Canadian capital, instructing aides and different legislators on his position in regard to the new wildlife protection laws which were to be enacted by Parliament soon.

"Now Mr. Prime Minister," inquired the leader of the Opposition Party, whom he had gotten out of bed at an early hour, "the law as it is being written affects the musk ox, the caribou, the polar bear...but what about the walrus?"

"What?"

"What about the walrus?" repeated the lawmaker.

The Prime Minister's mind worked furiously. A walrus! Could that have been the face he had seen through the periscope?

"Yes! The walrus!" exclaimed the great man happily. "By all means—include the walrus!"

Miss Lady

Once upon a time a sad little girl walked along a summer road.

She was about three years old, and she was crying because her brother was walking so fast she couldn't keep up, and then she stumbled, in a cloud of dust.

Her brother heard her cry but he kept on walking faster and faster and faster.

She was alone.

She looked over and saw a cottage and there was a man watching her from a window, peeping at her from behind a thick curtain, so she waved.

The face disappeared.

She walked to the back of the house, and there was another face, at another window, peeping out. She waved again.

And that face disappeared.

She climbed up on the back porch and knocked on the screen door, and after a few minutes the door opened a little. She walked in.

There were some men, and they gave her a Coca-Cola, and she talked with them, explaining about her sunburn, about her brother, and something about a trip to Canada her mother and father were going to take, and the men listened to her earnestly.

She hit one of them!

He picked her up and swung her through the air and she screamed! Then he perched her on his shoulder and she held his head tightly, afraid of falling, but then she lost her fear and just sat there, and they all laughed at her.

So she asked for another Coca-Cola.

One of the men got it for her and she insisted on drinking it out of the bottle; she sat on one of the guys' laps and listened, while the men talked of other things, taking great slugs of Coca-Cola occasionally.

Then she began prattling again and the men all stopped to listen to her. She asked one of them to fix her dirty stringy hair ribbon.

She played quite the lady and the men spoke to her with exaggerated English accents and this was wonderful!

Then she pulled one of them down on the floor and got up on his back and rode him like a horse, shouting gidiyap! gidiyap! gidiyap!

The little girl asked if she could come and live with them, and the men said sure!

So the men and the little girl got into a car and drove to Florida.

You see, these men were bank robbers.

The little girl loved it! She lived with them for eight months. She played on the beach with them, swam in the ocean, ate in big restaurants, lived in the best hotels, even drank champagne once! And she had a pretty maid who did nothing but wait on her and help her buy white dresses and orange bathing suits and all the toys little girls need.

They were always buying her presents and she loved them very much, but one day she got homesick and began crying for her brother and her mother and her father.

The gangsters were very unhappy but they bought her a ticket to her little hometown and they saw her off on the train. The conductor assured them she would arrive safely, which she did.

The police searched Florida for the bank robbers but they had flown to far corners of the globe.

The little girl continued her life with her family in the little town. She went to school. Much later she went to college; as a matter of fact, she attended Vassar.

2

Now she is a prostitute in Buenos Aires.

She is lying on a couch and her eyes are red from marijuana. Her clothes are lying on a chair. A sailor heavy-footedly leaves her room. She is so sad. Look! There is a tear on her cheek.

She is so pretty!

I can't help liking her. Because I know her secret, her quest, and why she lives this way.

I know she's looking for them.

Chess

Once upon a time there was a demonstration of Russian courtesy.

There is a fair-sized city in Russia, the center of a great gray barren region.

In this town there is a chess club, and anyone in the whole area at all seriously interested in chess belongs to this club.

For a number of years, there had been two old men who were head and shoulders above all the rest of the club members. They weren't masters, but in this area they were the chief players, and for years the club members had been attempting to decide which of them was the better; each year there was a contest, and each year these two tied. First one would win, then the other, and then they would draw, or stalemate. The club was divided: half the members thought one was superior, half the other.

The club members wanted to have one champion.

So they decided this year to hold a different sort of contest. They decided to bring in an inferior player, an utterly unknown person from outside the area, and each of the candidates would play him a game, and they simply assumed each of the candidates would win against the mediocre player, so there was no question of winning or losing: but rather they decided to vote afterward, after studying and discussing each candidates' game, and award the championship to him who played with better style.

The tournament evening arrived, and the first candidate played with the inferior player—until the inferior player finally shrugged his shoulders and said, "I concede. You obviously win." Whereupon the first candidate leaned over and turned the chessboard around, himself taking the position the inferior player had given up, and said, "Continue." They played longer until finally the inferior player was checkmated.

Then the second candidate played the inferior player until finally the outsider threw up his hands and said, "I concede." And the second candidate, exactly as the first candidate had done, turned the board around, and said, "Continue."

They played for a while until the harassed inferior player, looking blank, leaned back and shrugged his shoulders and said, "I don't know what to do. I don't know where to move. What should I do?"

The second candidate twisted his head around to get more of his opponent's view of the board, and then said tentatively, "Well, why don't you move that piece *there*." The outsider stared at the board uncomprehendingly, and finally shrugged his shoulders as if to say, "Well, it can't do any harm, and after all, what does it matter, as I know I'm going to lose anyway." With that gesture he moved the piece *there*.

The master frowned and pondered the board for several minutes before moving.

His frown deepened.

The corners of his mouth turned down.

His eyes hardened; he turned a sullen, stony, defiant stare at his audience for a moment before whispering in a choked voice all could hear, "I concede!"

He leaped up from his chair, raised his gold-headed cane quickly into the air, smashed it down onto the ebony and ivory chessboard, and split it in half.

He rushed from the room muttering loudly a long, strong string of profanities that were marvelous to hear.

He was, of course, awarded the club championship, and had, I think, incidentally demonstrated the proper way to lose a game.

The Blazing Blue Footprint

A footprint in blue ink from a birth certificate was blown up to the size of a football field, and projected in sections one night onto the White Cliffs of Dover by pranksters from Amsterdam, young artists. Ships in the Channel saw it, the bright blue footprint, reported it, and refused to enter the port when they could get no explanation of it on their radios. A squadron of RAF fighters swarmed around it. Three large naval vessels hovered offshore, and many men studied it through field glasses from the bridges, a blazing blue footprint. Finally landing parties were sent from ships in small boats, battling a choppy sea. Submarines surfaced and turned toward it, torpedoes ready, aimed at—"A blue footprint!" Helicopters swarmed down around it, and at first they didn't see the projectors, which the kids had taken elaborate pains to conceal, and the nearby town panicked—thousands left Dover that night on every available conveyance.

"Before I send you to jail," said the Dover judge to the dozen Dutch youths gathered in front of the bench, "have you any explanation as to why you caused all this commotion?"

"Your Honor," said the youngest-looking of them, "I traded my white bicycle for this document because I thought it was a grand thing to have, sort of a collector's item, you know."

He handed the document up to the judge.

"You see the footprint on that paper...a bunch of us were sitting around one night, studying it in a sort of admiring way, looking at it through a magnifying glass, and standing off and squinting at it from a distance, and I got the idea—it was my idea," he confessed, "I said wouldn't this footprint look wonderful—big as a battleship—flashing luminous on the White Cliffs of Dover. And everyone thought it was a beautiful idea, and so we did it."

"What is this!?" exclaimed the judge.

"It's a real copy of Winston Churchill's birth certificate."

"Do you mean that the cause of this was Sir Winston's footprint from the day of his birth?" exclaimed the judge.

"Yes, we thought he'd rather like the idea, if he were alive, and that it would make him laugh—"

The judge looked out over his spectacles at the London newsmen rushing out to the telephones.

"I shall have to give this case further consideration," said the judge. "This trial is postponed until after the weekend."

But the trial was postponed again, and later it was moved to London, and postponed again. The youths in London were invited to many parties and were soon in the swim of artistic society, several of them married English girls, some got studios and settled down to work, the youngest one formed a successful musical group—and the trial never did occur, although neither were the charges formally dropped, for to just forget is Justice when crimes are dreams.

The Purple Bird

Fluttering down of a purple bird to the plaza near the place where I sat in the sun each afternoon outside my hotel in Yucatan occasioned remarks in Spanish which I could not understand. The bird was as big as a robin, and was purple except for a white spot on its forehead and a baby blue breast. Six wind-worn umbrellas fluttered their tatters over tables in a way that in a cornfield might have frightened off birds, but this purple bird landed on a table one day and the waiter shouted something to his wife in the kitchen. She came outside with three plates in her hands and stared at the bird for a moment and immediately returned to her work, but from inside she shouted out, "Mi chinaca tompata que!" And the bird flew away.

On another afternoon the bird landed on the peak of an umbrella, and a nine-year-old boy, all dressed in white without shoes, sang out a song at the sight of the bird:

Chinampala talpo!
Se coro mular...
Chinaca tompata!
Me cora mular...

Or at least, that's what it sounded like he said to me, but I couldn't understand the words, and his Spanish sounded softly like Chinese as does the Mayan language. The boy had oriental eyes, was pure Indian with a classic Mayan profile, and he shouted out excitedly in Maya when he saw his parents coming, obviously telling them about the bird, and the bird vanished.

The next day, as I sat there, I spotted his flash of color up in a nearby palm tree, and I pointed it out to the waiter, saying the Spanish words for "The bird..." but the waiter didn't seem to understand me, and he stared a moment at the treetop obviously puzzled. The beautiful bird had hopped behind a frond out of view. After consulting with his wife, he returned a few minutes later, and waving to me, walked over to the tree at which I had pointed and, patting its trunk, repeated a Spanish word three times, obviously the name of the tree. I nodded, smiling, saying, "Thank you...thank you...," in English. A little later I glanced up at the tree and the bird was still there, moving around among the branches, but I didn't want to engage the waiter in another conversation. I left him a largish tip, for he was obviously being friendly, and had tried to help me.

"Simpala te quila!"

"Orozocar tamin...."

"Poche quinar?"

I had half-dozed in the sun at my usual table, and these voices mixed themselves with dreams. Only half-awake, I opened my eyes and beheld the purple bird perched on my knee. Without moving a muscle, I was instantly awake. The bird made a small odd sound and flew off to the tree. I stood up, and there must have been thirty people standing around me in a wide circle, all staring at me seriously.

I immediately went into the hotel. That evening, when I came downstairs, there was a flurry of excitement as I entered the small lobby to inquire after mail. Half a dozen people crowded a door that led to the kitchen, all of them staring at me with wonder in their eyes. A small girl tried to smile at me, but she dropped her eyes in embarrassment and stared at the floor. As I walked outside for an evening stroll, several customers of the restaurant rose from their table at the sight of me, and gawked.

Wherever I went that night, people were friendly. Strangers bought me drinks at the bar.

An old woman selling flowers fastened a perfect beauty in my buttonhole and laughingly refused to allow me to pay for it, chattering away in Spanish, saying the Lord knows what.

Continuing my stroll, I passed a group of young women outside a church who giggled friendlily and also stared at me.

I cut down a side-street as I usually did every evening on my walk, but tonight as I passed, people came out on their porches, and several waved a friendly greeting to me, and I waved back, smiling for a moment.

I had become famous in an afternoon.

I left the village the next morning and went into a different state to complete my stay in Mexico, because it's no good being famous...when people don't understand.

Real Magic

The magician on the stage dropped his glove. Yet he still held a glove in each hand. The elderly performer turned slightly, and as if by accident the glove in his left hand fluttered to the floor—yet he still held a glove in each hand. He looks at the gloves as if wondering where to put them down, and then puts them down on the table in full view, but at the next instant two new gloves appear in his hands. He puts these immediately down on the table on top of the first pair and flashes his hands empty so all can see with a gesture that would indicate that he is finished with the gloves, yet at that instant two new gloves appear in his hands. He takes both gloves in his right hand and places them over the back of an empty chair, and lo! there they are—and his right hand is empty, but two new gloves have appeared in his left hand. He takes the gloves into his right hand and flings them into the audience. In his hand outstretched from throwing the gloves, two new gloves appear. He also throws these to the audience, yet a new pair of gloves appears in his hand. He puts the right glove on—and invites a young member of the audience to touch one of his fingers as he spreads the fingers of his right hand wide. The girl touches his little finger. Without taking his other fingers or thumb out of the glove, he takes his little finger out, so that the little finger of the glove hangs limp. He takes a pair of scissors and cuts the little finger off the glove. He now pushes his little finger out of the hole so everyone can see. He then begins picking up all the gloves, and as he does so he shows the audience that each glove has only a thumb and three fingers; each glove has had the little finger cut off.

Members of the audience can be heard to murmur as they examine the gloves which he has thrown out to them, for these too have had the little finger cut off, although one person can be heard loudly protesting that when he caught the glove he had examined it, and that it had been whole.

The magician regained the center of the stage, and concluded with these words: "During the First World War, I served overseas as many men my age did and I saw a couple of battles. In one of them I was wounded, and at first I thought it was a calamity, for I had been left with a deformity which I thought to be grotesque and evident to everyone I met, one which was especially repulsive and tragic for a man of my profession, for I was then already a master of card magic, though I'd not yet begun to peform professionally. I then made a discovery which to me to this day seems truly magical—a discovery I shall share with you this evening, and if any of you are ever afflicted by a blemish or a sudden deformity I command you to remember immediately the message of my peformance tonight—that message is this: that when you work with people they really don't see your deformities.

"If you could have told me in my twenties that my deformity was going to be invisible I would have scoffed bitter disbelief; indeed, I would have found it incredible that one day I should with a certain pride display—as if I were doing a magic trick—the fact that long ago on a battlefield in France I lost the little finger of my left hand!"

He thrust out his left hand and held it steady so that all could see.

What the old man says is true.

And then as those old showmen could, with his left hand he waved them a gracious "Good evening!"

The Hunger of the Magicians

A stone lamp at an altar was lit by a flaming wand.

It was two thousand five hundred years ago to this very moment, in Greece.

It was a hot gray morning.

Overhead stormclouds are streaming by, but for months there's been no rain. Soon they will hear distant thunder, but still there'll be no rain, and very soon thirst and famine will finish them.

Out of saintly stubbornness they will starve to death, for they would not leave this place, this stronghold on Mount Olympus.

But now look! The lamp illuminates the lighter's face.

He wears a pointed hat.

Perceive the hat: it is two heads high, a cone, precisely wrapped by a single superbly cut piece—of gray stuff—heavy and rough, a giant swatch of undyed wool which falls from his cone to his toes, leaving a place for his face and hands to be free, forming a complete cloak.

It is the dress of a magician.

The master has a gray beard.

In his hands the light burns brightly. Look! There are fifty-two gray beards. The room is full of pointed hats. Their heads are bowed. All hats point to the lamp. It is a den of magicians!

In unison the masters moan in monotone the various vowels.

They wear no garment between their skin and their grotesque gray hats. Between their skin and their bones there is no flesh.

Here are the greatest magicians in the world, this is the Golden Age of Greece, these are the men behind that scene—but drought and famine have hit the countryside. The thrashing streams of Mount Olympus are dried up.

Nobody brought them any water or food.

And it made them mad.

Indeed, it was less than five minutes ago that the lighter of the lamp, the Young One, spoke up with a sublime assurance to his elders. This is what he said to them five minutes ago:

"The world is not going to forget this.

"I place the memory of this outrage inside the altar lamp.

"The sight of our miserable state shall rest here in the lamp until five hundred years has passed five times, until that veritable moment—and then it shall flutter free of the lamp and enter the head of a writer whom it'll madden for an evening, for he shall see us all here, and write it, and perpetuate this scene in the Literature of his language; and whatever language he writes, all the shining Literature of that language shall be transformed at that instant into lamps of rock more durable than this stone lamp, for that tongue shall survive to become the only language spoken on earth; at the moment when the vision flies, fifty-two writers of that chosen language shall become aware of the *hunger of the magicians*, they shall come as close to death as we are now; they shall witness vanity in horror and forget themselves: then Greek gods will be reborn; in them our light shall shine again; they shall refashion that language: new letters shall be added to its alphabet, and, as pigeon, it shall flutter between Hebrew and Chinese, and crystals of grammar in silver syntax shall be worked with ornaments from ancient tongues to transform it—they will make that language ready to write the history of the world; in their dreams they'll see what has duration in a language, and each in writing shall see a secret of perpetuity.

"I plunge my wand into the water, and...ah! I have speared a fish!

"Let us eat! Let us savor this moment of time.

"I plunge my wand into the fire. How quickly it catches!

"I destroy my wand to do this deed. This vision of us is our property, our land forever, and to sign the deed we must light the lamp.

"Magicians, great scholars, seers, if...it is your will?

"How brightly the tip of my wand flames.

"They shall see us everywhere, our quiet stare, in every line they write—a haughty mien, our silver smile of mercurial weight.

"For noon has come, and doubt is gone. There are no shadows anywhere.

"Now at last remorse surrounds the sources of our memory like purple light, the Godhead is bowed in blight...all our thoughtful frowns are snaked, our dragons are drowned, our lions are suffocated, our eagles are grounded....

"And if, when tomorrow comes with bells, Sorrow slaves at many works—then jonquils will be carried by canaries to this bright yellow spot, and sports will be performed by plants running on their roots, like a merry-go-round the great oak spins...and when, to a trembling touch, stone faces bend...petal-thin flesh shadows we can lift from the ground...bluejay's flash of sound....

"The sound of the seer is heard like a bluejay's shriek in the inner ear as it cuts crude consciousness away.

"Those fifty-two writers shall witness vanity in horror and forget themselves."

The stone lamp at the altar is lit.

Unpierced Pearls Strung
384 Unconnected Sentences
In Six Parts

For Charlie Morrow

1

This bracelet of unpierced pearls is strung by a marvelous method.

Their business is to transplant large old trees.

He corners a mouse with his three-cornered hat in a corner.

The first golf course in China comes alive with snakes an hour before the great earthquake at Tangshan.

An oboe player touches the pontoon of a seaplane with a dab of orange paint.

On the bottom of a shallow sea a scallop opens the mouth of its shell, makes a sound like a frog in falsetto on being touched by the deadly starfish, and leaps two feet through the water into the mouth of a rusted can.

An orange peel drops onto a corrugated roof from the same mulberry tree that later in the day will throw its shadow on the shed.

The Alpine greenhouse burns to the ground, leaving a gigantic black puddle in the snow, glittering with broken glass and floating ice.

A Note by the Author: Five sentences in this work were not written by me. Those sentences appear in Part 5 immediately following the sentence *Possessed by strange and friendly demons the author at the typewriter (writing this) changes bodies several times.* The five sentences were written at my request by my son, daughter-in-law, cousin, cousin once removed, and by my cousin twice removed—namely, by Sebastian Holst, Dawn Holst, Eleanor Jaworsky, Emileah Jaworsky, and by Laura Jaworsky.

There are sixty-four sentences in each Part. The first two Parts of this are an amended version of a piece which appeared under the title "Charlie Morrow's Bracelet," published in 1993 in Station Hill's *The Zebra Storyteller: Collected Stories of Spencer Holst.*

A Neanderthal child is pressing leaves and shells into the mud and removing them, leaving their impressions in the mud—making fossils.

He changes the direction of the stepping-stone walk.

A Caribbean team of deaf-mute scuba divers is successfully searching out sunken treasure.

I seek the secret of senility.

As she opens the furnace door, the blast of heat which meets her face melts her contact lenses.

They have no waterfalls in Holland.

The gong of bronze gone to verdigris is struck a thousand times by raindrops, while the peacock makes eyes at his mate.

Pressing the smooth metal tines softly against her face, she stares through the prongs of the pitchfork at the scarecrow she's been sent to dismantle.

Knots pop and pine resin drips and snaps in the hot wood fire—it is an original Franklin stove, built by Ben.

The sentence which follows will be really rotten. The sentence which preceded this was much, much worse.

Like a cork swimming madly to and fro in the foam of the swirling surf, a dead fish on which a scarlet butterfly prettily perches inevitably approaches—on gigantic indigo waves—the tropical shore.

The stationmaster stands, pocket watch in hand, beside the steaming locomotive, whistle in his mouth, waiting for the flash of the daguerrotypist.

The tongues of his alligator shoes are made from the tongues of alligators.

He smokes a Cuban cigar and wears a Panama hat and tells jokes on a nightclub stage.

She tries to look over the shoulder of the artist who is tattooing a blue butterfly onto her big toe—it's Whistler.

My Achilles' heel is killing me.

To have a black cat on one's lap, to have it yawn and gaze with great green eyes up at the candles that encircle the two of you as you illuminate the precious page with a giant letter in purple.

The bald man chooses a hat.

The first bird hatched from an egg laid by a reptile.

A white picket fence on which a teddy bear is impaled floats out into the center of a swollen stream.

Only a foot apart, 26 parallel white picket fences, each thickly covered with rose vines all burgeoning in blossom, stretch out before us for hundreds of yards—and from miles around come millions of bumblebees, each bumblebee a different word.

We slide along the salty walls of a tropical cave that's constantly swept by a strong oceanic wind, and we must stay alert to dodge out of the way of the large white seabirds flying toward us, that intermittently plunge through this narrow passage.

The saber-toothed kitten reclines in my palm, and its mother's paw rests on my outstretched arm: "A friendly beast..." is the conclusion the big cat has come to, though not in so many words.

Look further for whatever you find, get more of whatever comes easiest to hand, take it where such things are rare, and sell it wholesale to a shop.

At the poets' costume party all the revelers wear masks and sandwich boards; on the sandwich boards are written—hand-lettered, large and clear—the lines of poetry they most admire.

At the masquerade ball of the stage costumers all their outfits are made of tissue paper which are the actual dressmakers' patterns of their favorite theater costumes that have been cut out and put together with library paste at the seams.

Sunshine in Seattle seeps up from the soil through roots to stems and trunks of plants and trees, and is radiated by a billion leaves, lending the clouds, rolling low, that green glow.

Who hankers—should fetch.

They live an idyllic life in a houseboat anchored above a waterfall.

He made a million pesos on the icy mountain heights by opening a chain of shops selling to the Indians throughout the Andes paper cones of piping hot french fried potatoes—of a dozen different varieties.

A pink-eyed hound turns the corner, and stops to sniff at a chocolate tomato wrapped in red tinfoil that someone has stepped on.

He says he saw a silver buckle sitting on the table with its tongue out.

I gave her half my double Popsicle, and she shares with me her binoculars.

The out-of-work typist allows her fingernails to grow.

The fisherman who captures the Loch Ness monster in his nets as it gives birth to healthy triplets...

"This ain't turkey! It's tuna fish!" shrieks the condemned man on taking the first bite of his last meal.

The Scottish boy eats his oatmeal in a porringer, and he notices that his younger sister's hair is oranger.

The dog reverses itself in front of the mirror, and wags its tail.

A child drops a flashlight down the well—it kills a frog.

When will my collection of bottle caps become valuable?

The autumn afternoon rain hides a crescent moon from view, keeps crickets and birds quiet, and sends a frog under a leaf to sit, while over the pool the spider sat in his dripping web.

Tomorrow innumerable marbles will be shot with lines, sediments shall shift, dunes develop where the wind commands, clouds lace, and at midnight jet streams trickle to a stop in moonlit vast emptiness, again.

Broken bricks that fall about at the foot of a battered building (ancient work stopped) collide with half-cut stones in dust, and crabs run in and out; scorpions sun themselves in solitude while ants collect in cool caverns; sand collects in cracks only to be blown again by the wind, and by-and-by to fly again over the Gulf, there to fall, sinking into double depths, blank valleys of smooth sand, perfect as pyramids, perhaps.

What it must have been like to have been Balzac!

The thief who escapes up the flagpole steals the golden ball.

The touchstone is placed on the benchmark.

You're the only person in the world who carries the seven of diamonds in his back pocket.

I bequeath my brain, properly pickled, to the Literature Department of my old school with certain stipulations, which follow, regarding its display.

At the flower show he sticks his head inside the blossom of a gigantic morning glory and bites off its pistil.

Sometimes I write like a knuckleballer who's lost the knack.

I have more to tell, I've hardly begun—and you say my time is up!

When the wind blows from a certain direction, our windows rattle loudly—at such times it is hard to hear oneself think.

At certain times these small visions might assist one in getting from one moment to the next.

The grim reaper smiled at me, as has the muse of poetry—while listening as I read my prose.

This is being typed on cellophane.

My son went to Japan to study computers, and he returned in five years a sumo wrestler.

2

I have here this bouquet—a careful collection of dried weeds, each grown out from a crack in the cement.

The phantom buyer from out of state meets the secret seller from the inner city.

Hordes of handymen are hanging about with nothing to do.

The plainclothesmen are in fancy dress.

An ampersand unwinds.

A haunted jewel with a soul covers a cruel beauty's mole.

I fish for a name among my many noms de plume.

A nonce word is stuck under my fingernail.

There is a scintillator in my sock.

Whatever happened to the spoon with the long handle?

The ramp goes to an unmarked level.

He has a stopwatch as big as a saucer.

The most exceptional collection I have ever encountered is that collection of exceptions to rules, which prove those rules.

He believes in the rules of grammar but not in the Laws of God.

Narrow zeros make me nervous.

The man hops on one peg leg down the steps of the Mayan pyramid.

I push my way through autumn foliage of dense bush and underbrush until I reach the edge of a scarlet wall, I mean—a blazing moat, a gully full to the brim with a red river of poison ivy.

The horizon does not recede, but rather, as we approach, reveals itself to be the edge of an unfathomable abyss.

Beware when a megalomaniac acts like a servant.

Nerts!—once more, see if it can get through—Nerts! I believe it is something said in the thirties, let's see now—Nerts!—it is said by a young woman with a run in her silk stocking.

The tattoo of the blossom of an orange camellia sits on my arm like a bloodfilled spider.

She paints five-minute portraits on balloons and sells them for five dollars in the park.

On Chinese New Year the employees of the Hong Kong Botanical Gardens gorge themselves on snapdragon dumplings.

Fourteen cobblestones are missing from the street near the broken bridge where the old pimiento factory road peters out in an overgrown vacant lot.

As the ugly duckling returning as a swan, she cranes her neck to look back at the landscape of her childhood as the slow train brings her into the rundown outskirts of her hometown.

Imagine my tattered typewriter ribbon in this antique typewriter in a dilapidated museum.

In the hanky-panky of an Oriental afternoon an opium smoker shoots an Arab dancing girl for making too much noise with her bangles.

I see a dangler on my windowsill; it is my neighbor's monkey come to visit my gray parrot.

On a boatload of blue tile I am floating down the Nile.

He feeds a fast string of slowballs to a string of nearsighted batting champions at the Oldtimers Game.

There is a rogues' gallery in which we belong; there is a group of photographs which could be thrown on the table, and there— one of the photographs would be of us: the reader and the listener.

We aren't what we think we are, we really are what we pretend to be.

The dancer has two bad big toes.

I sincerely think you might have, though I hardly think that had you...

A swordfish has swum somewhat north in the Gulf Stream and is chased away from the entrance to a fjord by a school of narwhal.

There is a movie on every billboard.

Nature reveals splendor in various sizes.

We find a mushroom big as an umbrella that tastes like steak soaked in gin.

A pelican and a falcon land on the balcony of the Fish & Fowl Club, which itself is perched on the edge of a cliff by the sea.

The Paupers Club is an association of writers of short prose pieces that meets monthly at the old Anarchist Meeting Hall on Broadway below Fourteenth Street.

He found a fortune in amber and wastes it on jade.

A broken colloquium vanishes beneath the Virginia creeper.

The champion of sorrow has a horror of pride.

The unutterable demeanor of the big cat who is painted crimson from the tips of his whiskers to his tail by the gushing artery of a beached whale...

Great ghostly hordes of Indians are returning from the Happy Hunting Grounds, all vegetarians.

Instead of needles, the porcupine on awakening discovers itself covered with worms—"Now, you are mine, my pet," says Medusa.

The houseboat finds new freedom during the flood.

It will be a sign that the world is fundamentally changed when it becomes the fashion for ordinary people to wear shoes that don't match.

Notice the seriousness of that vegetable that knows it is to figure in a still life by the artist.

Ripe watermelon are visible by the thousands on the rolling hillside, and artesian wells send up streams of sunlight sparkling in the air.

A few waterfowl fly by the waterfall...my water mug holds a water bug.

I said seven solid silver seagulls, and I'll say it again—I'll swear to it in court: seven solid silver seagulls!

The Cincinnati ballplayer gets his chance.

They are the champions of chewing the fat.

Now she is thinking of what fiction writers talking to each other on the telephone laughingly refer to as "real life."

They dress their cats in silk.

The splendor of the invisible cord gives meaning to the knot.

It is easy to imagine having an elephant as a friend.

A dispute over dandelions becomes blasphemous and bloody at the Dublin Dandelion Winery & Bottling Plant, plunging the plumbers of copper tubing into bitter dispute with the coopers in whose barrels the wine is transferred from cold copper vats to be aged in old wood, prior to bottling.

There is something repugnant about a rusty funnel.

A footlong mosquito is buzzing at the window.

Going up the stairs at a run, up the 64 steps at the edge of the Ganges, hazarding a sacred saying at each step, imitating a holy man, the very devil, himself, in the form of a pussycat soaking wet from a fall into that filthy water, is transformed into a "vulture forever at the top of the stairs," and flies off toward the sun to soar on all the hot air there.

A chocolate brown Burmese show cat sits quietly inside a brown paper grocery bag, pretending she isn't there.

Imagine you're in my movie, and this is your close-up: the camera comes to focus on your hand, your hand fills the screen in the elegant theater, and the camera slowly circles the hand revealing the changes of positions of the fingers which are grasping an object that is at first mysterious, but then turns out to be a book: the fingers are grasping a book...and then, miracle of miracles, there is a soundtrack to the movie being shown in the elegant theater, and the room in the theater becomes filled with the sensitive sound of a throat being cleared, and a quiet cough which is not at all ugly, and obviously precedes the sound of spoken words...ah, the words are the author's...but it is my reader's voice that is heard in the elegant theater on the sound track of the movie, my reader's voice.

3

Here is Sherlock Holmes in my garden! and I say to him, "I'm a first line writer...."

There is a way through Sydney to the marketplace of birds, where cockatiels and parakeets are sold, down Winthrope Street to Nordens Knoll, turning north on Tasmanian Boulevard into Eucalyptus Lane.

A violet is eaten every morning for breakfast by a vivid violet lizard.

"Thanks a million for the fiver!" sang out the livery driver to the foreign-office fool intently bent on a fool's errand.

My cat plays the dulcimer, her dog plays the harp—together we could make beautiful music if only they could agree on what is *A Sharp*.

I'd like a quarter-pound of cold anomaly.

While saying everything, he insinuated nothing.

So what would I say, were I to be asked? I would say first—that I should be last.

"What happened to me hedges? begorrah, they were eaten last night by the hedgehogs!"

It is the perfect poison which makes the victim's death an excruciating happiness.

Clouds of orange smoke and pearl gray ash arise from an idling pool of bubbling magma on the first moon of Jupiter.

You think it's an accident that a walnut inside its shell looks like a human brain—it is no accident at all—walnuts are smart.

"Have you ever started a landslide?" asks the famous villain of the movies—at a cocktail party—of his famed competitor from the rival studio, the Infamous One, so-called.

The skeleton key is carved out of bone and it fits a crystal lock of a music box, whose parts are quartz—the whole thing being transparent.

The piano-playing gym teacher choreographs a silly exercise on a sisal rug for drum majorettes at the bidding of the high school principal.

A silver nightingale being painted by a Chinese Sung master reflects the firelight on the cradle where the baby lies in the shadow of its mother's chair.

It is always my ambition to type a sentence from one edge of the paper to the other, and then some.

"More dots...more dots...more dots..." is what the muse of painting whispers in my ear.

The jack of diamonds is a no-good, a veritable knave, a hard card to hide in your shoe, for if you try to, it'll eat a hole in your sock.

There are quiet interludes in certain gardens when flowers tinkle in the breeze as if made of the finest antique porcelain while, like jazz musicians, several mockingbirds compete.

The tattoo artist and the plastic surgeon are a team—their ex-patients form a club and exhibit themselves at The Museum of Far-Out Art.

A hair-raising hailstorm assails the tin roof of the mail room, destroying the equanimity of the post office cat.

I have a cat who talks to me while I typewrite what she says—she says she wants to learn to type.

In the warm, pouring rain, oh! the slippery black desolation on the bare obsidian mountaintop.

Their maroon pickup truck backs into the outside corner of our wooden garage, breaking its taillight while turning around in our small backyard.

The unicorn wears the cornucopia as a hat.

Dipped in viscous, dark orange mucilage, the chopstick is thrust into the large keyhole and the protruding stick chopped off.

She can lift one eyebrow and move one ear like a cat, making her eligible to train for admittance into the secret society of women who know how to purr.

To be apt is the opposite of being vague—an artist is apt to be vague.

A surge of salient factors bedazzles the analyzers.

The nine year old studies the dashboard of the unfamiliar car.

Stretching out across the black iron belly of the wood stove the black lace firescreen gently balloons before the embers.

He has the heart of a fence.

I relegate to an inferior the job of correcting my mistakes.

I am the incurable optimist who will die in despair of ever getting well.

It is but a commonsense precaution that rabbits who live in top hats should beware of ventriloquists.

On my pond I sail a gondola of gilt between its silver boatshed on the shore and my sleazy gazebo on an island where gray gladiolas grow to the exclusion of all other colors—but then it is so far away—now so long ago.

Nobody could go past the door without his shouting to be let out.

People without money walk in slow motion.

A tulip from the palace of the Czar is given to the sleepy boy with the sore shoulder by the cook's daughter-in-law.

The marbles tumble out of the shoe into the grass.

An imaginary headache saves his life, for if he had gone to the poetry reading it would have been the death of him.

My portable typewriter, with its handsome letters and characters—we could go places.

Arising out of nowhere, the first thing I do is tie my shoe.

A curmudgeon lost his tongue for saying *orange sponge*.

Dusty windowpanes piled inside the musty garage near the innertube and crusty paint cans serve the black widow to support her web.

Lemon noodles hit the ceiling.

He draws a circle in the sand, and says, "This is the universe, and now imagine ourselves as two giant four-dimensional creatures, capable of rational thought—or at least, that is—capable of imagining things."

He is making what he calls Hodgepodge Hootch when by accident he stumbles onto the formula for the Mysterious Mixture.

First I step on someone's toes, and now I get on someone's nerves.

During a decade of cooking for the kids she has saved and dried 500 wishbones from chickens and turkeys and each has been covered with glue and dipped in glitter, each fastened along a long, long string, which has become the only decoration on her Christmas tree.

Woolibooliwoolichik!—now that is not real writing.

At least if I were falling, or had been flung, on one wing fluttering, trying to rise above some obstacle—perhaps the garage—oh then!

The dogs that ate the goat begin to growl and howl.

He's the kind of guy who pays too much attention to his cats.

His lordly manner causes him to be arrested.

She is a long phoner, a mad mooner, a long-gone loner, and she doesn't speak English.

The porkpie hat falls into the gumbo soup.

Death is deaf in one ear.

The new customer at the manicurists' shop has ten balloons of flesh on the tops of the tips of her fingers, instead of fingernails, spheres of skin the diameter of silver dollars, filled out taut with a phlegmy foam.

He sleeps on a horsehair mattress and has a featherbed for a cover.

Now the hair on my earmuffs begins to grow as fast as my beard.

Bad poetry can be good prose, thus: Halfway to noon from dawn, that is, at nine I begin to yawn, and soon to dream that I get a dressing down in rhyme from a clown in a dressing gown that's mine.

Let flowers fall from baskets from balconies to bridesmaids, frogs leap into countless pools to break a single silence, fountains play into the air now caught by sudden ephemeral rainbows, pigeons fly from belfries preparing for the gonging, flowers lean their heads listening to the breeze, and yet I shall follow your shadow forever, flickering about in the sunlight.

4

My only other book is *The Negev Desert Highlands Handbook.*

In northeastern Texas four inches of hail as large as tennis balls falls on the cornfields, pommeling the cattle grazing on the hillside, killing the crows that have been sleeping on the high-voltage wires, devastating the greenhouse, transforming the lawn of July which surrounds the farmhouse into a winter wonderland of snowballs which will melt in half an hour.

It is a giant Pacific Ocean Frog, a species well-known for its island hopping.

The prisoner places the bucket of water in the corner of his cell, sticks his head in the bucket, and then stands on his head until he drowns; and in dying his body does not wildly writhe, but remains erect, upside down, until rigor mortis sets in.

I am the needle in the haystack that can never be found, which has lost the thread forever.

The melancholy mongrel whose companion cat has died—leaving him the only animal in the house—frowns, snuffles, and grows especially moody when it rains.

He carefully cuts out the dots over the j's and i's and mixes them with periods, colons and ellipses—he throws them onto a piece of aluminum foil, folds the foil, and from it pours them onto a blank page of a sketchbook.

A cobalt blue glass basket containing a fresh orange, a lemon and a lime floats on a pool of mercury.

I would not cry out in the middle of the night, but should shudder in the dark.

She puts her shoes on the wrong feet, wears the cups of her bra over her shoulderblades, and puts her dress on backward, for only in this way can she enter the hall of mirrors and retain her identity.

An anchovy shaped like a starfish falls on the folded napkin which rests on the plate in front of the King of England.

Hand-over-hand up the ladder, foot-above-foot, without a thought as to what it could be like coming down, finally reaching the top and sitting on a burlap bag, legs extended, hands on my lap, I scooch myself forward over the edge of the giant slide at the fun house, an exquisite pleasure I can vividly recall sixty years later.

I found this amulet in my omelette when unexpectedly (my car broke down thereabouts) I took a meal in the kitchen of a Scottish castle.

The gumshoe gets what's coming to him on April First when his two young daughters glue his three pairs of shoes quite firmly to the closet floor, glue his jackets to their wooden hangers, and his hats onto the hat rack.

One might easily imagine that an author puts a clean sheet of paper into the typewriter, and types several lines which, though not untrue, are unremarkable.

The hen pecks at the eyes of a potato.

He is the dunce of donkeys.

There is nothing more special, or more unique, than the serene dot over the j that sits so securely between the accent marks in the phrase *déjà vu*.

Hearing a distant scream as distinctly as the drip of the faucet, certain people work late on into the night until the small hours, and create their own provenance of quietness.

A go-cart is mounted in the front and back of each Indian canoe, so that the wheels protrude through the stretched skin hulls, and Canadian teenagers race them from lake to lake along the long-suffering trappers' old trails.

He has a brogue on each foot, and you can never understand what he's driving at.

In a melee the police move like a school of fish.

Sometimes it is merely that one is unique, and lives a life below a swallow's nest.

He is indeed an old geezer from Gander.

What is the name of the gnome on your nose?

Send a poet on a poet's errand, send a fool on a fool's errand, and send a Bengal tiger to Bengal.

My Reader, if you should suddenly discover that you have this very vase in your hands, handle it with care and a certain circumspection.

After all this to land on a landslide.

He opens her change purse and there is nothing in it other than the Perfume of Drunkenness—he thrusts his nose into the purse and inhales deeply three times...and then outside in the street is arrested for drunken dancing.

Fat flat feet in tight shoes sliding down a hill of gray gravel in a gay dance of the might-have-beens...

You aren't really talking to me, are you? says the Reader to the Listener.

In Salt Lake City the Mormons have begun to kill each other off, completely without reason, it having something to do with religion, according to the FBI, who have penetrated that organization.

A pig in a nursery rhyme mates with a pig in a Dickens story, and their offspring now all work in Hollywood.

The fandango is not a dance invented by God, nor yet is it the work of the Devil alone.

The northeasterliness of her nomenclature boggles southwestern minds.

She shivers on her stalk, an awkward orchid in an arctic garden.

A quiet claim on the silences between the chirps of the katydid is held by the woman who takes her pleasure in the way words are put together.

Three thoughts on the badger: 1.—oh! but these are unthinkable things!

The daylong drizzle develops into a dazzling downpour with electrical displays accompanied by the roar of subway trains—instead of thunder—drowning out everything.

The Cornish hills are calling...long distance...there is a whistling on the line...an ancestor from long ago wishes to speak to his great-great-great grandchild...you bear that title, you know.

Chinese poems do not rhyme, nor can sonnets be translated line for line.

He will cook in the same restaurant for seven years.

There is a farfetched beckoning from the unfathomable—I shall return presently—goodbye.

"The flower that stands alone in the vase, it is I whose voice you hear—all my countrymen are slain, and I, also, soon shall die—let me tell you where the buried treasure is!"

Riffling and dovetailing, fanning and double-cutting, dealing from the bottom—the fifth ace....

He has chocolate socks, a bamboo sweater and elephant-ear trousers.

An old man in olden times might have a mammoth for a pet.

She is a nameless nobody, a perfect character for a fable.

Over a cold shoulder he boldly throws the warm cloak of the absurd.

We'd spared the leopard double jeopardy.

I hold her glasses between my teeth, while she presses her lips against the windshield.

He has a rash of tiny wounds that do not close or heal.

He orders roast chicken delivered from the dozen nearest restaurants, giving his next-door neighbor's name and address—the next thing the madman does keeps me from writing anything more about him, yet I can't help but think of all the things he's going to do now.

His pitchfork is missing a tooth.

She fixes her hair with a scrub brush. The muse's muscles ache with yearning for greater literature—she sits on a cloud with her elbow on her knee, and her chin in her hand, and taps her foot on a floating puddle in time to the music of the prose writer's typewriter, making splashes.

A rain of punctuation marks are falling on a beautiful sheet of bond—100% rag, if you know what I mean.

For a sporting spat I put her Pekinese pup on the purple rug beside my Siamese cat.

His collection of lemurs roams about his house all night, being without exception nocturnal, as he is, and they sleep all day in their cages.

I dread the shock of walking up my block and finding everything as it was 35 years ago.

When I married my stepmother's daughter from a previous marriage, my stepmother became my mother-in-law.

A hidden treasure is regularly knocked about in boiling water at the bottom of a samovar.

There's a bathtub in the tugboat, and in the bathtub there is a toy tugboat, a perfect replica of the large ship.

The three-pound brilliant toad is hopping mad, exuding a different toxin from each pink, violet and orange spot on its glistening skin.

5

Filled to capacity with bombastic politicians, noisy millionaires, professional gamblers, jazz musicians and raucous showgirls all loudly engaged in the various forms that wild laughter can assume in furious midnight revelry—with a drunken captain and negligent crew—the magnificent Mississippi riverboat slides through the somber midnight silence of dense fog and inadvertently misses the Port of New Orleans, enters the Gulf of Mexico, paddles turning through the night, not landing until noon, when it drifts ashore on an unpopulated part of the Yucatán Peninsula.

The only time I saw him his head was underneath the hood of an automobile.

Poor Baudelaire takes a boutonniere from a bush of blazing azaleas.

My father always exaggerates things, and my mother speaks in hyperbole.

Usually I type using only two fingers, but today I am striking the keys with two sausages.

I am the reincarnation of Fred Astaire's sister.

On some days there's nothing to do but stay home and write.

She pulls a fricative out of the sand and hurls it into the ocean.

Her pekinese pisses on our pool table.

A cat is chasing sandpipers for food on an uninhabited island.

An icosahedron decides which triangle to lie on.

The million-dollar movie stars a two-bit actor whose name is ridiculous.

For months he rides alone through the mountains in a double-decker bus.

A pack of hounds without a master races through the forest.

The man with the ultraviolet flashlight shows the way.

He steadies himself on a stalagmite.

An orange lollipop is stuck to this page.

There are intermittent lightning flashes in the ice cubes.

The gray cat without fur can wear pearls with aplomb.

The eerie squeal of the singing eel...

She calls the lumberjack lambie-pie with a French-Canadian accent.

The Duchess of Daiquiri looks like her dachshund.

More caterwaul than doggerel, more overall than general...

I dance the trocadero in my head.

Lemon fragrance over bushes flushes white butterflies from shadows.

She gets a sinking feeling as the elevator rises.

My neighbor owes me nothing except silence, and I wish he would pay up.

What is the opposite of dancing?

The thing about dunces that is most attractive is their hats.

A tripod for a movie camera falls off a cliff.

A pale opportunity is approached with gusto!

Pointless, unpoetic, redundant—at my age—a horrible haiku!

A vine twines around the leg of the scarecrow that is decorated by morning glories.

Hopeless night coughs flag attention to a slab at the morgue.

A path of floating steppingstones leads to an unmarked grave.

Cringers are put through wringers.

He stands up in a canoe and waves a bright yellow flannel shirt.

I spend the evening in the overstuffed chair surrounded by his books.

The shoemaker wrenches his shoulder shoveling snow.

I cross my fingers and fold my arms.

Forever forward without elbow room.

He rubs his eyes with his fingers, and thirty things run through his head.

Not a vestige of a beginning, no prospect of an end.

He collects limericks in a cigar box.

I like to write a sentence that rattles.

My sister hit me with a sleighbell and broke a vertebra.

The librarian loses her index finger.

Possessed by strange and friendly demons, the author at the typewriter (writing this) changes bodies several times.

The juvenile gypsy jumps the jailer—the tiny medium is at large.

She is spoiled by her genius, her brains have gone to her head.

A decrepit fence is dressed in ragged diapers and worn-out jeans.

The ax murderer buries her victims in the petrified forest.

Does spun sugar ever shatter?

She forgets which is which.

Ovals belong in an oblong.

Pumpkins hang in the grape arbor.

He hides the flagpole in the well.

The glimmer of a halo glows dimmer in the shadow of a horseshoe.

Her whiskey voice has a husky touch as she trills her r's in a Scottish burr the Nova Scotia way.

The fallen-off particles from the summer picnic table of the young Copenhagen physicists on holiday in northern Norway are devoured with alacrity by gigantic arctic ants.

Seventeen goats wander single file down to drink in the mist, at the foot of a sky-high waterfall.

A freakish storm blows a flock of flamingoes, brown pelicans and blue herons out into the mid-Atlantic, where they land on a rudderless lifeboat containing ten children who are using their sailor hats to bail out the boat.

The North Dakota marching band wears purple uniforms with yellow plumes on their hats, grass-green boots and long red underwear.

Filled to capacity with 200 youngsters all shrieking out of sheer delight and glee, the ferris wheel is rolling free—down the boardwalk and the beach, barely missing us as we loll in the sunlight and sand—it is followed now by numerous policemen blowing whistles and a horde of screaming parents...and *here they come!*

6

I don't want to be cremated—I want to be a fossil, my features perfectly preserved in stone of different colors, perfect as a Roman citizen in marble, my whole body good for five hundred million years, a fossil forever!

The daredevil who cut off the ear of the Oriental millionaire art lover who stamped his vermilion seal of ownership onto his recently purchased ink drawing by van Gogh was never apprehended, was I?

Sixty-six screaming Alaskan ice skaters are thrown off balance by an earthquake that sends a single crack across the ice on the lake, and that crack can be seen from above to continue across the land for several miles on either side of the lake.

He throws a harpoon at a raccoon sitting on a Mississippi palm tree and almost kills Mark Twain who is lying there in a hammock that is tied to the tree, reading over a sentence he's just written.

The jumping jack leaps out of the pack of playing cards at a gesture by the conjuror and it is precisely *that card* which the spectator has chosen at random and returned face down into the deck: it is the jack of spades—is it not?—the one-eyed one...what! you chose the four of hearts...oh.

The child weeps when the string of his robin's-egg blue kite breaks at sunset, and the kite sails on into the cloudless night, startling a pair of lovers when for a full minute it hovers in front of the full moon and then crashes at their feet.

A would-be round-the-world balloonist, en route for take-off from an air field in New Jersey, got stuck in a truck in the Holland Tunnel where he died of a number of things: of claustrophobia, of desperate disappointment and finally (fatally entangled in his parachute cords) of carbon monoxide poisoning.

In a tug of war between *three* two-toed sloths and *two* three-toed sloths, each group gets a grip on one end of a vine held twenty feet up in the air between two Cecropia trees that are twenty feet apart—and the contest continues twenty hours until the liana breaks, and the five tumble to the ground, and then tentatively on each of the five faces a very slow smile breaks.

A household lives on a houseboat—a California seagull lands on the windowsill, and can be seen through open slats of a closed venetian blind, and now his wife smiles in her sleep, hearing his voice whispering to the purring cat, punctuated by a buoy's distant ding-dong, and by the Sausalito Harbor seals that have just begun to bark at dawn.

I smile to myself as I watch from the porch the mailman approach with a letter bomb in his pouch that someone unknown has addressed to my noisy neighbor, who regularly plays his stereo after midnight, with the bass turned up to boom.

Flaming applesauce comes out of the spigot and caramelizes the surface of a scoop of vanilla ice cream which rests in a cut-glass cobalt blue bowl inside an antique pewter holder, one for each person at the first-class luncheon on the ocean liner S.S. *Song*, crossing the Equator on the Indian Ocean, headed for Madagascar on the way from Bombay.

"If you don't recognize me, officer, I guess it means you haven't seen any of my pictures—I'm Philip the Fourth."

The marine beast she caught on her sharkline is a gigantic Portuguese man-of-war whose longest tentacle measures 48 feet on the floor of the taxidermist's workshop, where soon it is to be stuffed, and mounted, so that it can be permanently displayed over the bar in the Harbor Tavern, of which she is now the sole owner since the recent death of her husband in a storm at sea.

The dozen countertenor midgets of Mindanao performing with the ten giants of Java singing bass in conjunction with the Borneo Boys' Choir are taking European concert halls by storm.

In Trinidad eight tap-dancing shoes have been exquisitely made to fit like gloves on the eight feet of two Siamese cats who have been trained to tap atop a dozen steel drums to tunes made popular by Fred Astaire and Ginger Rogers.

In a gold box the old artist collects the white hairs that grow from three warts on his long earlobes, and when his collection gets large enough, one day he will use the hairs to make the perfect watercolor brush.

When she raises one eyebrow, and one nostril rises into half a sneer, and one eye closes to a slit—*watch it!*

At the operatic debacle, the rising note of the screeching soprano cracks the baron's rimless monocle.

Sitting in the sun there is a sensuous silence that gumchewers know—with closed eyelids—who are below age ten.

The ugliest curves a man can envision are those bendings in slow motion of a tornado seen in the distance.

She lies in a casket of quicksand which she heated to improve her complexion, and it cures her arthritis.

This sentence is rushing across the page, and being written by a prose-writing drummer typing with two fingers, hammering an old manual typewriter going rat a tat tat, rat a tat tat, rat a tat, rat a tat tat tat tat tat tat tat...tat, and an orange flower appears out of the blues.

Two miles inland south of Lake Okeechobee a helicopter founders in the swamp, sinks three feet and sits there until three Navy frogmen (in dress uniforms, not in wetsuits) are rescued by children in canoes from a nearby girls' camp.

Tryouts are treats for showoffs.

When you walk upstairs you get older, when you walk downstairs you get younger.

In upwind storms on the downslopes of the cone at the volcano's peak—cinders fall in the snowfall, lightning ignites the ice on the cliff, and through the high bursting clouds brilliant small eyes of orange magma peek.

A thousand frying pans of different sizes hold a thousand different recipes for sauces at the Joyous-Ginger-Cook Convention this afternoon in Bangkok.

Between the snow line and the tree line where mountain goats and mountain sheep hop about, where dolomites delight geologists, where the lame mountain lion has his den and his own domain, where limping lightly rock to rock he reigns, eating mostly mountain mice...

When the wind is from the west our well emits a low whistle or a soft howl like a lost soul or a loud owl.

I think the only orange dining room tables that exist in the Americas or Europe are lacquer antiques imported from China, except for this table, on which this typewriter sits, on which this sentence is being written.

Beautiful drawings of three hundred and eighty-four snowflakes, all accurate renderings of photographs of actual snowflakes in all the glory of their variety and sixfold symmetry—can you imagine a different snowflake beside each of these 384 sentences of the Bracelet?

Among the various kinds of artists, the author is preeminent among quick-change artists.

Sugar maples are planted on both banks of a meandering stream which cuts the yellow elm forest in half, so that in autumn a scarlet line defines the path at the river's edge.

Shadows gurgle in millstream shallows where guppies rattle speckled pebbles by the moss-covered log, and the giant carp bites the toe of the lazy salamander.

As my fingers tap at the typewriter I feel tiny metal letters one-by-one strike against the inside surface of my cheek, and I taste the ink—I taste the word.

A mickey mouse band performs with abandon—it's a night when what is worst is best.

The doghouse of the airedale on the terrace of the penthouse cannot compare in elegance with the abode of the orange cat in the greenhouse, who sleeps in a basket among orchids in a climate that on the coldest nights is never anything but tropical and sweet-smelling.

As other birds develop gallstones, large red rubies grow in the gullets of ruby-throated mockingbirds.

She knows her husband will lose his head drinking jack-o'-lantern punch—for tonight is Halloween—and so for her own costume the seamstress sews together a dozen men's hats to make a handsome dress for herself.

Probably there are more barons than there are monocles.

Many sheets of newspaper are hung out on the clothesline in the rain, and each sheet has been folded in half and fastened by two clothespins, each being the front page of a different Oriental newspaper, each in a different language from the others.

In pouring rain, dawn arrives in the dark today.

The secret of making perfect fudge is imparted to a 14-year-old girl by her bald-headed bachelor uncle, who had learned it from her long-deceased grandmother when he himself was fourteen.

Nobody knows what the painter sees.

Crossing the stream in a cutting style, the steely stiff-legged pair of scissors pirrouettes in the moonlight on each steppingstone.

Incredulous, they stare down at the horses where the forces of the Mongols wearing slanted goggles gallop beside the Great Wall to the beating of the gong of Genghis Khan.

From tattered tartans she makes patchwork kilts for Scots who have four grandparents that each belong to a different clan.

Near that double-hairpin S-curve that causes a driver on that highway to cross the Great Divide three times in as many minutes—there at the side of the road a sweet potato blossom meets a morning glory on the way up the fence for the sun.

A collection of wildflowers is gathered at dusk for the dinnertable by my wild grandchild.

My job is to furnish live snakes once a week to the Toledo Zoo—summer and winter—which they feed to their famous collection of mongooses, nine species in all, and the most complete collection in the United States, and that includes a family of rare snow mongooses from the foothills around Mt. Everest, which have white fur and are the only mongooses that hibernate.

Each of five stunt men auditioning, one after the other, inadvertently it would seem, falls off the stage into the orchestra pit headfirst into the kettledrum, hovering for a long moment upside down and upright, standing on his head inside the drum, revealing trembling legs that waggle wildly, adorned with purple and orange striped socks; but none of them does it good enough, and the playwright on the spot rewrites that part.

Full moon blazing, four jaguars swim the Amazon to an island on which large tree-climbing nocturnal lizards congregate to feast on the eggs of numerous nesting long-legged birds—jaguars dislike the taste of lizard and find the birds too difficult to catch and lacking in flesh, but are irresistably lured by the bodies of two plump sweet-smelling BBC cameramen, who are also attending this lurid midnight lunch.

The telephone man left the wheezing customer's house in a huff, for the sick old codger had contrived to engage him in a hand of poker and one thing had quickly led to another, and he lost fifty dollars before he knew it, and then he found that the phone he'd brought to install didn't work; but when he returns in an hour with a functioning phone there is an ambulance in front of the door—a neighbor has discovered the body—and the paramedics note that if he had been able to telephone for help they might have saved him, but now the old codger lies on the floor with fifty dollars clutched in one hand, and a dead phone in the other.

"What is it?"—the dinner guests are fascinated and their hostess is transfixed as a caterpillar slowly drops on a silken thread from the glittering crystal chandelier to the centerpiece of apples on the dining room table during dessert, and a lady with an English accent answers—"Malacosoma americanum."

All the farm machinery in the field is turned brilliant orange with rust, weeds grow tall as sunflowers, the farmhouse is a wreck, the barn a shambles, panes of greenhouse glass all broken, bare skeletons of animals litter the yard, and thousands of black birds roost in the giant oaks that have no leaves—after fifteen years the murderer has come home, and is examining three tombstones that lack words on their faces.

The king of the deep forest around the Brazilian town of Tefé (near Lake Tefé, which is fed by the Tefé River) is a twenty-foot fifty-year-old boa constrictor—the King of Tefé, he is called—and now with single-minded tenacity the Amazonian constrictor squeezes and tightens his grip, and then chokes to death trying to swallow the fifty-year-old obese chief of police.

In sprinkling spring snow the very last gigantic Irish elk breaks the ice crossing a shallow stream, rears up on its hind legs, and teetering a moment, falls over on its back upon the ice—and scrambling awkwardly, rises to its 11-foot height, looks around and then majestically gallops off down the stream bed breaking the ice as it goes, leaving a path of hoof-holes which a four-foot prehistoric Irishman follows, carrying a spear with a sharp tip of chipped stone.

A wealthy dwarf wanted to furnish pleasant well-paying employment for others of his size who were not as lucky as himself, and so he designed a Garden of Giants which would be entirely cared for by dwarfs on ladders, a garden that specializes in growing and selling giant varieties of flowering vines, plants, bushes and trees of a thousand different species, which are now consuming amazing quantities of water daily and are continually fed fertilizers; the place has become a popular park in which to wander, people pay to enter it, pay the dwarfs big money for the big plants, and the enterprise is altogether successful—and it has made the wealthy dwarf a happy man.

In a busy section of the city six hundred glass eyes have been carefully arranged in pairs on a huge piece of crumpled black velvet (each pair is a different size and gazes in a different direction) in the storefront window of a successful taxidermy shop, and there are no other things in the window, no stuffed animals or birds, but there are amazingly almost always at least a dozen pairs of eyes on the other side of the glass, just looking.

Three tons of iron weapons fell to the floor with a terrible clatter at 2 a.m. in the Armor Room of a California museum at the advent of a modest earthquake; the museum's collection of Indian pots rolled around in their glass cases, and neither cases nor pots were shattered; and though ten thousand books were tipped off their shelves to form long piles along the museum's library aisles, the only thing actually shattered was the equanimity of the pretty girl who (according to museum curators) has the world's most beautiful white whiskers, the museum cat, who at night was left in charge of the place, and who, according to a laughing Mexican museum guard, is a Mexican god—the Jaguar Earth-goddess—and is the one responsible for the earthquake.

The tumbledown shack on the mountainside in the middle of a meadow of wild grass and wildflowers at the side of the tumbling rapids and a small waterfall where cardinals and bluebirds abound and in the evening bats and swallows surround and fly in and out of broken windows and doorways open to the weather, where in the winter a grizzly bear hibernates, making a nest of the bones on the bed of the long-dead owner of the house, the hermit who happily got to die in his own bed.

In a small movable shed at the center of a frozen lake at noon in northern Minnesota a successful ice fisherman plops another fat fish onto the pile beside him and again drops his line into the hole he has drilled through the ice, while from out of a much larger shed at the shore the racing iceboat *Snowbird* emerges and sets its single sail for speed, and from the other far shore, banks of freezing fog emerge in lobes, moving out in tongues of zero visibility which soon force the iceboat to a complete stop at the center of the lake a few feet from the shed unbeknownst to the fisherman, and the two sit silently surrounded by northern Minnesota's largest pack of wolves, who can smell the blood of the fish.

Haresbreath is a minute orchid of Northern Australia with tiny blue flowers and white leaves and stems that grows in the air out of rotting limbs and on the ground from rotting logs whose curious flowers are said to open within a hairsbreadth of dawn, and are known not to open at all on overcast or dark rainy days, and in a tropical room of the Great Greenhouse at Kew Gardens in 1846 were observed by Charles Darwin to close during a solar eclipse.

The Cincinnati ballplayer got his chance at romance when his wife through an ordinary accident became afflicted with amnesia and then fell in love with him a second time, as if it were the first time; before leaving the hospital the chaplain there married them again, her doctor gave the bride away, and they returned to what had been their home for a number of years, yet for her it was an entrance into the house of a stranger, for she did not recognize the place nor any of her previous possessions; and those strange possessions of a stranger held for her a sacred fascination and— not knowing what to do with them—she cherished them, and for forty years they lived on in that house, and it was as if the old house itself and those strange possessions of the stranger held the secret to the mystery in their long and happy marriage.

About the Author

SPENCER HOLST is of old American stock (Celtic-Scandinavian-Indian) which has produced four generations of writers. His first American relatives arrived with the Massachusetts Bay Colony in 1630 and were among the founders of Windsor, Connecticut. "Their ship," Holst says, "became iced in on the Connecticut River forcing them to spend that winter eating acorns.

"My sister, Marry-Ella Holst, and I are the only Ohio writers born in Detroit, Michigan.

"My great-grandmother founded a newspaper in Ohio soon after the Civil War, the *Weston Avalanche*, and my grandmother received the Hattie Award from the Ohio Womens' Newspaper Association for writing the same column for sixty-eight consecutive years, and my father Doc Holst, also a columnist, was a lifetime member of the American Baseball Writers' Association, covering baseball in Detroit, and much later writing for the *Toledo Blade*, the Ohio city in which his three sisters lived. My mother wrote for many, many small newspapers.

"In the geography of literature I have always felt my work to be equidistant between two writers, each born in Ohio—Hart Crane and James Thurber, but my wife says don't be silly, your stories are halfway between Hans Christian Andersen and Franz Kafka."

For years, Spencer Holst has had a devoted following based not only on his three popular collections of stories, *The Language of Cats, Spencer Holst Stories*, and his collected stories *The Zebra Storyteller*, and wide-spread magazine publication, but on three decades as the storyteller *par excellence* of New York's literary cafés.

Holst is a recipient of the Rosenthal Award from the American Academy and Institute of Arts and Letters and an award from the Foundation for Performing Art. He is also a painter and lives in New York City with his wife, the painter Beate Wheeler.